girl

girl

Camille Laurens

Translated from the French by Adriana Hunter

OTHER PRESS

NEW YORK

Originally published in French as *Fille* in 2020
by Éditions Gallimard, Paris
Copyright © Éditions Gallimard, 2020
English translation copyright © Other Press, 2022

Production editor: Yvonne E. Cárdenas
Text designer: Jennifer Daddio / Bookmark Design & Media Inc.
This book was set in Goudy Old Style by
Alpha Design & Composition of Pittsfield, NH.

1 3 5 7 9 1 8 6 4 2

Library of Congress Cataloging-in-Publication Data
Names: Laurens, Camille, author. | Hunter, Adriana, translator.
Title: Girl / Camille Laurens ; translated from the French
by Adriana Hunter.
Other titles: Fille. English
Description: New York : Other Press, [2022]
Identifiers: LCCN 2021045577 (print) | LCCN 2021045578 (ebook) |
ISBN 9781635421019 (paperback) | ISBN 9781635421026 (ebook)
Subjects: LCGFT: Fiction.
Classification: LCC PQ2672.A78365 F5513 2022 (print) |
LCC PQ2672.A78365 (ebook) | DDC 843/.914—dc23/eng/20211006
LC record available at https://lccn.loc.gov/2021045577
LC ebook record available at https://lccn.loc.gov/2021045578

Publisher's Note
This is a work of fiction. Names, characters, places, and incidents
either are the product of the author's imagination or are used
fictitiously, and any resemblance to actual persons, living
or dead, events, or locales is entirely coincidental.

To my wonderful daughter

one

1

"It's a girl."

It starts with a word, like light or darkness. Your birth is like the creation of the world, and there is heaven and there is earth, one word cleaves space in half, splits the masses in two, separates time. It's not God who pronounces it, though—better for you to know that right away. It's Catherine Bernard, a midwife at the Sainte-Agathe clinic where the clock on the wall says it's a quarter after five. She didn't prepare this announcement, she didn't want or determine anything, having all the less opinion on the matter because she's a nun, but the result is the same: she says it, she labels you as she brings you into the world, there in her immaculate headdress this virgin bride of Christ pronounces her judgment, she gives birth to you by labeling you. You're born from this word as if from a rose, you bloom in her mouth. You're still nothing at this stage, barely a subject, struggling to come to life; you can't yet say "I am," no one says "she is," not even in the past tense, "and the girl was," even with an indefinite article—"and a girl was"—it's not something people say. You're not indefinite, anyway, oh no, you weren't born indefinite, there's already an "s," you see, just one tiny letter to make the switch from he to she, but a huge letter all the same. In fact, you're a very definite article. The facts speak for you. Born a girl. There it is, it's been said, it reverberates in the room, a white space with a bottle of water, a small bed, and a crucifix. Your birth is a commonplace enigma. You're almost nothing when you're born, it's all a little rough-and-ready. Some schism is taking place, but where? And there is evening and there is morning. The one follows the other, the one becomes the other. But not you. You can't be changed. That's how it is. It's too late now for the fairies to gather around your crib. The deed is done. You arrive in this world headfirst and your newly delivered life unfolds in the free air, well, "free" in a manner of speaking because day or night, morning or evening, you won't be anything else ever again. You cry, you scream out loud, it's a cold hard truth filling your lungs, a feminine rhyme, and the crying gives you a harsh sense of separation, you can feel a division, it's as simple as that, there are now two, there's a cut, it's cut. Your birth separates you both from your mother, who's also a girl, that's a known fact, and from all of humanity that isn't labeled a girl. The opposite word isn't spoken, and with good reason, but it hovers silently in the ether of the room, the inverse word creates a stencil effect in the air, until now the embryo, the fetus, the baby had been "he" or, at best, "it." She or he, only a few seconds ago everything was still possible, grammar could still glide dreamily over the landscape, but now your wings have been clipped (and what else?), you're more alone than Robinson Crusoe but still, it's done, the die is cast along with the placenta. God (who was born a boy, people say, who was the father of a son, people believe), God is a child who plays dice: it's a girl.

"It's a girl."

The voice that formulates your incipit has no particular inflection other than the modulations induced by a job well done. Catherine Bernard likes a little drink when she's not on duty, but her results haven't been affected to date. She's helped plenty of women become mothers, oh yes, and brought so many fruits of their wombs into the world. Even when really probed, she wouldn't reveal a preference—an ambivalence at most: newborn boys always remind her of baby Jesus in the manger, the sacred aspect of her work and of the nativity. But girls are less alien to her, she finds it easier to wash them. On reflection, she realizes she spends a lot of her time fiddling with genitalia. Baby boys' parts are huge in proportion to the rest of their bodies, inflated with hormones, they're all anyone can see. With girls, where they're more discreet, she feels less shame, even though that's ridiculous. Lord, forgive me my thoughts.

"It's a girl."

On the other end of Sister Catherine's announcement are your parents, its recipients, and its guilty parties too, the girl-manufacturers, the troublemakers—in the zero hour, which of them failed to supply what? But right now, that's not the prevailing question, although later they might blame each other in order to ratify their disappointment, to deal with the intransigence of it. So, they receive the news. When they were waiting for it to come, waiting for you to come, they knew nothing. They didn't see you through the opaque walls of your mother's womb, didn't watch your hands stirring its liquid air on a glowing screen studied by someone in a white coat. Someone whose practiced eye they would have eyed eagerly, clinging to a decisive statement always clouded in some doubt (for the sake of professional conscience), touched by such intimate interpretations (to be moving about that much, this must be a...)—hanging on the oracle's pronouncement, on the likely truth of it, not "It's a girl" but a more cautious equivalent, an approximative synonym: "I can't see anything." They weren't informed of your missing configurations in the specific place where this matter is configured. "I can't see anything," by which you understand: "It's a girl…" Nothing to see here, move along please, it's a girl. Your parents didn't expect or hear such announcements because the appropriate equipment doesn't exist yet. It's 1959. A shadow of the family jewels— or nothing—pixelating before the viewer's eyes has only just been conceived as an idea; technology isn't yet inscribing the thickset waves of longings and disappointments, no image captures amniotic swimmers, so you can go to great lengths, you can move heaven and earth with your kicking, but the suspense remains intact to the end, and your "hello there"s with your toes are wasted, despite all the pregnancy predictions: no morning sickness, it's a boy, can't stop throwing up, it's a girl; soaring libido, it's a boy, zero sex drive, it's a girl. Craving salt, craving sugar? Girls like their food, everyone knows that. They say that if the bump is as round as a soccer ball, the baby's a boy; if it's shaped like a rugby ball, then it's a girl. ("Pah!" says your grandfather who tricked the All Blacks in 1925 in a stadium full to the rafters.) There are still more secret hypotheses, whispered from ear to ear by laboring women, in between two bouts of panting: if you orgasmed when the baby was conceived, it will be a boy, if you didn't feel a thing, you're having a girl. Your mother's worried.

It's news for another reason too: you're not the first. It's not just a girl that's being announced to them but another girl. A second girl—second and final they're thinking, not anticipating any more (they're wrong). You're not just a girl, you're a girl *again*. You follow on from a girl. Your sister (you'll soon become aware of this), your sister was born before you—and with your birth, you're the one who gives her the name "sister," you're the one who baptizes you both with a label other than girl, the label you now share of sisters (she doesn't want it, mind you, and neither do you nor anyone else). By the grace of God, your elder sister was allowed to come into this world without too much haggling. Still, she was named Claude just to let God know (not that anyone believed in him) that, well, they were expecting, they thought, they hoped . . . You, though, the second girl, you're bewildering. "It's another girl": you're disappointing news. You weren't expected. Your sister didn't set things up well for a pigeon pair, but you've made it a couple of lame ducks.

Your father's taken the trouble to be here, all the same. Full of impatience, he attends your birth. It's still very unusual, ten years before May 68; fathers are kept away from their wives' dilated vulvas, from the pain that stirs smells of shit and blood in them, from the way they moan like dying animals as they empty out their innards. The fathers would never get over it, so people claim, the sight would make them impotent. Men are protected from a bankrupt libido and couples from mutual disgust. But an exception has been made for your father, he's deemed strong enough to stay in the delivery room, after all he's in the business...well, nearly: he's a dentist. So he's used to gaping wounds, then, not horrified by bloodied mucous membranes. Being accustomed to gums, he's unlikely to feel threatened by a vagina with teeth. Unlikely to pass out on the spot, gelded for life by the terrifying spectacle. Every day, he...Wait, what? No...It's not your father who's a dentist, what nonsense, that's Dr. Galiot whom he came across earlier in a billow of cigarette smoke along the corridor, next to the midwives' station; he'll be your dentist when you have teeth, and the son he's about to take in his arms, without even putting out his cigarette, will be in the same class as you for eighth and ninth grade— Jérôme Galiot, a little asshole born the same day as you, your not-twin whose cheap jokes will help you understand just how opposite the opposite sex can be, but for now he's his parents' trophy at the Sainte-Agathe clinic in Rouen, just fifteen minutes and a few centimeters in length ahead of you. No, *your* father's a GP on the rue Jeanne-d'Arc and he already has a name for you: Jean-Matthieu. Jean like his father and Matthieu like himself, honoring the men in the family and the two finest Gospels, an expression of puritanical Protestantism. He was contacted at his office and told it would be soon, he dropped everything and came running then left again, then came back at five in the morning, the night air nurtures the XY chromosome, it'll come right this time, it's a boy, he can tell, he wants to be there. He waved to Dr. Galiot in passing, "Congratulations," and hurried into the delivery room just as you emerged from the abyss. Sister Catherine feels lukewarm about the intrusion, she makes a sort of draping action with her apron as if she's been caught naked, and your father hardly has time to see you crown before she dispatches him toward your exhausted and still-ignorant mother: no room for jealousy, and it's more seemly. Judging by the scant hairs stuck to the top of your head, you're of the male gender, for sure, it could even be said there's no mistaking you're in your fifties with galloping hair loss and not long left before you'll be bald: your father's joking but no one's laughing, your mother's demented with pain, the fruit of her womb is raking through her, she'd forgotten this monstrous pain, she'll never say a word about it to you because pain is erased from the body's memory more readily than pleasure, nature's a clever thing, and you'll experience this supreme torture meted out to the girl-born soon enough. Your father stands by the bed half-heartedly holding the mask over your mother's nose, and her want of oxygen and tenderness, while she strains her neck toward Sister Catherine who's immersed in the struggle of new life, "come on, push, come on, breathe," hoo, hoo, and back to that, and on again, the shoulders are out, how many babies has she given birth to in words? The moment of delivery is near, meanwhile your father—as he waits to hold the baby, or at least the truth about this baby—holds his breath, he suddenly loses faith, strangulated and lost for words as he teeters on the brink. "What is it?" your mother asks between two gasps for air, no one knows yet, one last push, there isn't a smell of roses and yet there it is, your father falls apart, did he ever believe otherwise? What is it? It's a missed opportunity.

You're laid on your mother's stomach, hi there, says your father when he sees your undeniable vulva. You cry. On autopilot, he breaks into a smile, then backs away. You're not mewling, you're yelling, screaming, what a pair of lungs, funny that, you couldn't tell the difference from the sound of it. A booming voice, 3.9 kilos, 52 centimeters: we came so close. Your father leaves the room. It all feels exhausting to him, he's empty, goes home to bed—the cord, the first feed, the first bath, they don't mean much to him, in four hours he'll be giving consultations again. And calling the family in the Ardèche, carefully modulating his rasping voice: "It's a girl . . . yes, yes, that's nice too." A girl. There, it's said, it's done. The champagne can stay in the car. With a boy he'd have watched the first bath for the pleasure of seeing those favored body parts float. But a girl . . . nothing to see. It's not that he's unhappy, no. There's just a little something missing from his happiness. He slinks along the walls to avoid seeing Dr. Galiot again but bumps into him on the way into the parking lot. "Well?" "It's a girl." "Ah! That's nice too."

"It's a girl."

Come to think of it, perhaps those aren't really the first words you hear—because you do hear them, that much is indisputable: it's not known exactly what new-born babies can see, whether they're more or less blind or shortsighted in the first few hours, but no one has ever suggested they're deaf. It's even said that they hear sounds in utero, several months before they come into the world, that, through the gurgling and whispering of amniotic fluid, they can make out their mother's voice or its reverberations, the father patting her stomach, when there's a father around, and music if it's played loudly enough. In your particular case, your father certainly made no effort to engage in conversation before you were born, it's not like him to talk to strangers—male or female. It's also unlikely that you heard Bach's cantatas or Mozart's sonatas because he listens to records late at night, at a time when a pregnant woman should already be in bed. On the other hand, in the mornings and afternoons, when your father wasn't there, your mother listened nonstop to that year's hit, "Only You," crooned by the Platters, *"You're my dream come true, my one and only you,"* because she'd bought the single the day it came out. Or Doris Day singing *"Qué será,*

será, whatever will be, will be" ... So perhaps, before that inaugural sentence, during your multilingual gestation, you caught snatches of bottom-of-the-swimming-pool English, and would translate them later when that became your job, only then understanding "*You're my dream come true*"; and possibly a few words of Spanish muffled as if by earplugs, "*Whatever will be, will be, the future's not ours to see.*" The last of those lyrics are more fitting to the happy event than the first because what happens is categorically not what anyone was dreaming, given that what happens is in fact just you, in other words it's only you. Six months before you were fully developed, then, you were all ears, ready to listen, firstly to the refrains of your future existence and then, on the cusp of the outside world, to both the plop of a pebble skimmed across the relatively smooth surface of the surrounding silence ("It's a girl") and its ricochets bouncing from voice to voice ("That's nice too," "Better luck next time," "Girls are easier," "You'll just have to keep trying").

You're swaddled in a white sleepsuit, a present from your grandmother who didn't want to tempt fate. Have you heard the one about the two babies on the maternity ward? Two babies have just been born and they're lying next to each other in the hospital's nursery. "What are you?" one of them asks, "A boy or a girl?" "Don't know," the other replies. "Hold on," says the first one, leaning toward the other crib, lifting the blanket, and peering in. "You're a boy." "How do you know?" the other one asks. "Well, you're wearing blue slippers." There was a degree of caution with you, they resisted knitting anything sky blue, decided against painting the walls periwinkle, refrained from hanging a navy frieze in the nursery that had been readied. A little patience with that azure. Never count your cockerels till the eggs are hatched. But they didn't tend toward candy, salmon, or blush either, they even avoided eggshell in favor of pure white, snow white (virgin white) onto which fate and chromosomes could project some (blood) red or (royal) blue: it's nature, not our dreams, that writes the story. The presents offered to the new arrival soon make up for this hesitation. Rabbits, rattles, hats, towels, you'll have a *vie en rose*, pretty in pink—like that dress of Grace Kelly's that so many women have copied since she married her prince. Even the safety pins holding your diapers in place will be pink—yes, you're born at the historic frontier between washable and disposable diapers; and that doesn't make you look any younger, I know, I know. And, can you believe it, this white layette doesn't do your mother any favors, it wasn't really a brilliant idea. Your grandmother's knitted enough for six months, what with the sleepsuits, the blankets, the cardigans and socks, all in neutral white, so every passerby in the street, everyone in her apartment block, and every patient of her husband's who takes an interest but has nothing to go on has to ask "What is it?" or "What's your baby's name?" and your mother has to keep replying "It's a girl," or even (and this takes the cake) to disabuse anyone amazed by your misleadingly sturdy frame, "No, no, I promise you, it is a girl."

Your father goes to the records office in the morning to register your birth, to register your presence in the world (your presence with its significant absence). Confronted with the registrar, he can't remember the name they'd chosen if they were unlu–, if by chance, in case... What was it again? Juliette is Romeo's other half, his appendage, well, there's no appendage on her, ha, ha! Juliette is ground zero in the wiener department, she's all about waiting for what she herself isn't, for what she doesn't have, she's a girl's suffix for life, that patronizing -ette that makes things small, feminine, and cute—brunette, rosette, statuette, dinette—Juliette is a diminutive made girl, a perennially diminished Julie, the girl languishing on a balcony, a paltry rhyme for an embittered poet, making the hero Romeo shine implicitly by his absence. It has to be said, your father's family name is Barraqué, a relatively unusual name but it sounds just like a common word for muscular, beefy, brawny, hunky, stacked, built—that's quite the patronym, the sort of name that gets you a son, a stacked Jean-Matthieu. But given the circumstances the onomastics have him stumped—and they're not going to make your life any easier, by the way. So then? Nathalie? Annie? Sophie? A serenade of silent "e"s, a tango of mute little girls. Martine? (Tell me another one!) Jeannine? Hmm. Josette? No. (Phew!) He's all at sea. He finally remembers a film he's just seen at the movie theater, *The Prince and the Showgirl* with Marilyn Monroe and Laurence Olivier. The showgirl was Marilyn Monroe. Marilyn then? With an "e" to make it more French. Marilyne. Not bad...But what if you grow up ugly? What if you don't develop a decent handful? Marilyn's not a gift. It puts quite a weight on the bearer's shoulders. And her breasts, and her derrière. (And, anyway, Marilyn Stacked...yeah, right. Your father's not actually a total idiot.) It's like Juliette but in a different vein: too in-your-face. Why not Carmen, while we're at it! And what would Simone, your mother, say? It would be like giving her a rival in the crib. The prince, on the other hand... "Baby's name?" the registrar asks again. Laurence Olivier...Plus your father looks like him, several people have told him so. (And Sean Connery too. And Tyrone Power, a bit.) Laurence Olivier. Dark and brooding, like him. A priest's son (an Anglican one, but hey...), a wonderful actor (he even played Romeo). Suspected of being homosexual? Your father doesn't know, he doesn't listen to malicious gossip. "Laurence," he says. Laurence from the Latin *Laurus*, "(covered in) laurels" (your father has no great knowledge of etymology, but he's a doctor, he knows every plant by its Latin name). You'll be a Greek athlete, a

Roman tribune, your forehead wreathed in leaves. You'll be Spartacus, you'll be Romeo, you'll be Caesar, Apollo, Napoleon if need be. You shall be a prince, my girl. At least those *rosbifs*, those Brits, will think so. You'll be Laurence, the perennial laureate—and there you go, another silent "e." No one can say your father wasn't conciliatory the day you were born, acknowledging the silent "e," accepting that powerful "s" that made the transition from he to she. ("She or he! SHE or HE! I can't be bothered with this inclusive nonsense," he'll tell you sixty years later. "Women are already included when you refer to men.")

Later he returns to the clinic with your sister, Claude, who hasn't yet grasped that you'll be coming home with them, but she still can't see what's so fantastic about you and why everyone's going into ecstasies. The main points are: Uncle Albert's mouth (poor child), Grandma Marcelle's nose (thank goodness), feet far too big for your age (twelve and a half hours), and slightly slanting eyes although no one knows why. Two slits in the middle of your face: you look Asian (just don't mention Mongolia—yes, people said that in those days). "I asked the midwives why my baby looks Chinese," your father says to entertain the gallery (and in an attempt to gloss over his memory lapse at the registry office). "They said something about neonatal jaundice, genetics, and the will of God: I wasn't convinced.

I pressed the point and then they said, 'We could run tests, we'll write you with the results, so check your mail, man...' Aha, I thought so!" Everybody laughs except your great-grandma (who goes to the post office later to check). On hearing your name, your grandmother intones "Law-runs?" and wrinkles her nose. Why not Florence instead? "Flaw-runs?" your father asks. So you'll be paired with a city? What a thought. You'd lose your laurels, you'd no longer be expected to accumulate them on your head, like a man. That would be a shame. "Looks like I need to wait a while for my rugby team, then," your grandfather says, giving your biceps a feel all the same.

You're a girl. It's not a tragedy either, you see. You are slant-eyed but we're not in China. We're not in India. In India the words "It's a girl" are now banned. Saying "It's a girl" before the baby is born is punishable by three years in prison and a fine of 6,000 rupees: people are no longer allowed to ask for or carry out scans to identify the baby's sex and then have an abortion, and this is because too many girls are vanishing; so many have been nipped in the bud that there are whole villages of single men. So many girls have been liquidated, they never use the words "sister" or "wife." Before scans were invented girls were killed at birth. If you'd been born in India or China, you might be dead. In Rouen everything's fine. You're loved in spite of it.

You might reply that in some parts of the world it's the other way around: in Mexico, among the Zapotec people in Juchitán de Zaragoza, there are huge celebrations when a girl is born because women are the head of the family and pass their name on to their children. Men hand over their wages to their wives, who manage the household accounts. But, well, that's in Mexico, and even then, it's only in one tiny corner. Meanwhile, in your household, your mother has no bank account and isn't allowed to write a check or to work without your father's permission—she doesn't work, in fact. She does the cooking (very well, she's been to housekeeping school), she plays tennis (well) and checkers (moderately well). The tennis is tricky, your father's not in favor because of the tournaments that take her and her short little skirt away from the big Sunday meal, which ends up being thrown together or left entirely to him to manage. She'll soon make the most of her idleness by taking a lover. That's the system that girls in our country have found to assert their freedom, on a par with the boys. *Only you* can come in a variety of forms, *Only you, and you, and you.* Watch out, boys, two can play at that game. The female of the species is more deadly than the male.

"It's a girl."

It starts with a word, like light and darkness, like the darkness extinguished by light.

Now, you may hear this word a lot, coming from Catherine Bernard then from your mother on the telephone, her face very white against her pillow as she spreads the news; you may hear it a lot from the very first day, but you don't necessarily understand it. Well, of course you don't understand it. The word "girl" means nothing to you, no more than the word "boy," which sometimes pops up in your mother's conversations. Gradually, with the passage of words, you'll grasp its inaugural significance. You'll understand that, despite what that "It's" might lead you to believe, this is no neutral observation, no statement, but also and rather more emphatically a position in relation to the world, a destiny in counter-relief, so to speak. What "It's a girl" means first and foremost is "It's not a boy." But before you know this, you'll need to learn other words.

You meet your family. By ear and then by sight, and touch. First of all, there's *Mommy*. *Mommy*, it's the first word you learn and it's a girl's name. It would be the same if you were a boy, you'd keep up your mantra of *Mommy* just the same—*Daddy* comes later, it's a proven fact. Boys and girls all love their mommy first. Love is a girl, when it comes down to it. Skeptics claim that it's the first word simply because it's easier to pronounce. Mmmmm is what lips do naturally when they're rooting for the breast. A bilabial consonant that lends itself to the mumblings of hungry newborns. Mommy is basically yum-yum, they say, it's the classic mammalian call confirmed by phonetics.

Love is a breast, when it comes down to it, nothing more. Yes, but it's a girl's breast. Rounded, swollen with milk, nourishing. Daddies don't have those, you'll notice this. You're already noticing. When your daddy picks you up, there's nothing to latch on to under his white shirt, it's all flat. Nada behind his tie. That must be why he never picks you up. Would he pick you up more if you were a boy? Probably not because, whoever you are, at this stage you're just a dribbling baby. And anyway, boys don't need cuddling so much. It softens them. Still, the question's there. Besides, Mommy's always around. You cry, she shows up. You're hungry, her breast appears. You poop in your diaper, she cleans you. You stink, she covers you in nice smells. Your teeth hurt, she gives you your giraffe teether to chew. You're afraid of the dark, she switches on the night-light. And all relatively quickly. Daddy, on the other hand, does absolutely nothing, you notice. You also notice that Mommy's voice is softer and more tender, she says kissy-kiss, peekaboo, sweetheart, there-there, and sings soft words that send you to sleep. The deeper voice—that you'll soon associate with all hairy, flat-chested figures that have lumps in their necks and wear pants— has more inquiring inflections: All okay with the baby? Where's my shirt? When are we eating? By and large, the daddy voice asks a lot of questions and the mommy voice answers. As a general rule, Mommy's body is here now, you walk around with it, in its arms you discover the kitchen, the bathroom, and the bedroom, whereas Daddy's body is somewhere else, beyond the door, out of sight. The daddy voice isn't addressed to you, it refers to you, occasionally, almost scientifically: diaper rash, breast pump, vaccine shortage; whereas Mommy's voice helps you associate words with things, sensations, and actions: crib, bath, kiss, hot, beddy-byes, love. The daddy concept is an absence, Daddy's not around, whereas Mommy is. And if she ever doesn't reply, another voice picks up the baton, a voice paired with breasts and dresses, that goes by the name of Grandma or Nana or Auntie or Ginette, a soft, attentive voice—obviously other girls' voices. A syllogism is imprinted in your brain's signage system: love means being there. Girls are there. So girls are love. Mind you, your sister is the exception to this rule. She wears dresses and has a tinkling voice, but she's not often around and when she is you don't feel safe. So you can't be sure that your sister's a girl. To be confirmed.

On the subject of girls, there is one strange fact. You're a little girl, that much is clear. But you're also your father's little girl. And your mother's little girl. Some languages, but by no means all, have the luxury of the word "daughter," but in many—and French is one of them—your sex is not distinct from your relationship to your parents. You will only ever have this one word to describe your being and your lineage, your dependence and your identity. A girl is forever affiliated, she never leaves the family. Dr.

Galiot, on the other hand, had a boy and he had a son. You have only one entry in the dictionary, he has two. The phenomenon is repeated later: when you grow up you become a woman and you may possibly also become a wife. Again in some, but not all, languages this distinction doesn't exist: *femme* in French, *Frau* in German, and *γυναίκα* in Greek mean both woman and wife. This single word to identify you is a constant reminder of the yoke you bear, you're always seen in relation to someone else— your parents or your husband—while a man exists in his own right, language itself says so. Grammar lessons will teach you this later, in your little school for girls next door to the school for boys: the masculine always takes precedence over the feminine, so a group of fifty women and one man would be referred to as *ils* (they, masculine) not *elles* (they, feminine). You'll have to learn this by heart at some point, but you know it from the first day. Just in case you haven't memorized it conscientiously enough, the preacher will explain it again, using stronger imagery. God created Adam and then, thinking he looked lonely, He fixed Adam up a partner from one of his ribs. Eve was created from a scrap of male rib cage! Seriously! You've pictured gooseberry bushes and swallowed the story about storks, but girls and women born from a man's bone, no. That's going too far! You and your sister giggle on the way to Bible study: "So is Adam one rib short? He's not in great shape, then, this ancestor. Boys don't check all the boxes." And at the time of your confirmation, when you're fifteen, you ask anyone who's prepared to listen, "Hey, girls, you know why God made Adam before Eve? Because before you make a masterpiece, you have to make a rough sketch." And all the catechumens burst out laughing. The preacher, on the other hand, doesn't think you're ready for your first Communion that year. You don't take it. You never do. Jesus isn't a daddy's boy, you don't give a damn, and you have the balls to say so. But we're getting ahead of ourselves.

You were born several weeks ago, and you're home. Your sister, Claude, watches you suckling lustily. As she peers into your crib with a feigned smile on her lips, she'd cheerfully drive a knitting needle through your pupil, but Mommy keeps a weather eye open. Every day, you suck your mother's breasts for all you're worth; nestled in the crook of her arm, you know no greater pleasure than vacuuming in this white liquid that's restocked in response to the whims of your crying. Apart from your sister who's keeping tabs on you, and all the pink crowding into your field of vision, you experience no grounds for dissatisfaction. Your happiness lasts for four months and then, for some obscure reason, your mother sticks something strange into your mouth: a rubber nipple with a hole in it. The milk it supplies doesn't taste the same and, more significantly, your mother is a completely separate entity from it, you can see her busy chatting on the phone at the far end of the living room, while your grandmother or Ginette, the cleaner, gives you your bottle, and sometimes you can't even see her at all, she's not there. Has she had it with you dragging at her breasts four times a day, threatening to ruin them? And what *would* happen to her if she stopped being beautiful? What happens to ugly girls? Or does she want her schedule free, liberated from your rapacious timetable, even though she doesn't work? Because staying home with two young children isn't work, everyone knows that.

The truth is there's another reason. Your mother's pregnant. What? Again! Yes. Your mother implicitly believed your father's reassurances (he's the scientist, he knows how this all works, women's bodies have no secrets for him): so long as she's nursing, she can't conceive. It's mathematical. Lactation prevents ovulation. Sure, right! Your father's a whiz at contraception! Unless he sneakily reverted straight to his male ambition: to have a boy. Your mother doesn't have time to catch her breath. And you don't have time to ask for more. You're weaned on the spot—cut-and-dried. Weaned from your mother's breast and her arms. She's still around, but she's resting. It's because she's carrying a baby, that's what people say. But it's the exact opposite: she's not carrying you anymore. You're left stranded on the carpet, in your bed, and in the bottom of your rocking chair. You don't understand any of it.

You feel like a forgotten doll, something unsold on a shelf, a piece of tat abandoned at the prospect of a new arrival. What's wrong with you? What does this new baby have that you don't?

Your mother's waters break on a Friday afternoon when she's at the movies with André, a friend of your parents. Luckily, he has his car and takes her to the clinic, not waiting for the end of the movie. Your father continues with his consultations, he doesn't make the trip, preferring to hide his hopes behind the telephone receiver. What is it? It's a girl.

And then there were three. You couldn't make it up.

She's called Gaëlle. Which is written Gaël for a boy, and even for a girl (but don't make a thing of that, your parents are not on first-name terms with Freud). In the end, it's just for the registry office; no one has time to call her by her name because she dies two days later. "Poor little scrap," your grandfather murmurs. You know nothing about this, of course, your grandparents are looking after you and you don't understand the word "dead," you're only thirteen months old. There may be no trace of your dead sister in your memory, but the same can't be said for your *black closet*. So at the end of the corridor at your grandmother's house there's a windowless room, a sort of storeroom that everyone calls the *black closet*. It contains a chaotic accumulation of unidentifiable things and you can only ever get past it at a run, without stopping, because

you're convinced it's home to monsters. The thing is you
have this black closet inside your head too. On November
15, 1960, when the ashen Gaëlle stops breathing at the
Sainte-Agathe clinic, there's already quite a mishmash inside there, bottle feeds that didn't go down well, Claude's
knitting needles, your mother crying, your father's chin
wobbling. But Gaëlle herself takes up residence in there in
royal style. The total darkness doesn't bother her, quite the
opposite. She becomes the child in the closet, the secret
victim of some terrifying Bluebeard. "We kill girls here."
You race past the sign as fast as you can, without looking,
you'll read it years later when you've learned to read. Is
it there because you killed her? You so badly wanted her
dead that you're terrified by the strength of your feelings.
Another sister? Absolutely not! That would bring an end
to your glorious reign. You'd be obliterated! Hunkered
down in the black closet, your hatred is performative.
So she took the breast from your mouth? Down with the
stripling! She ousted you from your mother's arms? Let
her die! You bombard everything with your evil thoughts
and now look, fate has granted your wish. Or there's another, not so dark version: your mother didn't want her—
another child when she'd just fallen for André? Terrible
timing. Or perhaps it was your father, who only saw her
when she'd died, not deeming it urgent to visit his youngest daughter, *ter repetita non placent*, by the third time, it's
lost its allure. In short, Gaëlle, the third daughter, the last

sister, didn't land in the right biotope. No one wanted her, so she slipped away discreetly, and girls don't need to be taught how to behave like that; she just had to embrace her decline. You won't be going looking for her in the black closet. That's enough girls. Good riddance. Exit the little scrap. But later, and for years and years, every time you cut something up—bread, a cake, cheese, anything— you cut a tiny extra slice, one more than is needed, a little nothing of a scrap, and you put it to one side, even if you do always end up eating it yourself. You don't know why you do it, but you can't help yourself. In spite of every- thing, this *little scrap* celebrates your cannibalistic jealousy or the remorse inherited from your parents: it's the angel's share, Gaëlle's share.

Right now, you're crying but no one comes running. As you grow you make yourself smaller and smaller, you don't want to be any trouble, or to notice that no one goes to any trouble for you. You stop crying, behave as if you don't need anything (so long as mealtimes aren't forgot- ten). Your parents look as if they're at a funeral, and you've been buried alive, and you sure deserve it: you should have just been a boy, they'd have found it easier to swal- low the disappointment of your sisters. Your baby sister only dies once, while you . . . You die in your mother's gaze because she no longer sees you. You die in your father's regret because he no longer believes it possible. You die in your older sister's jealousy, yes, she's still dreaming of making your day. You even die in Gaëlle's death because you can't replace her. All in all, you're not at the party. You would experience every death meted out by childhood if your grandparents didn't breathe some life into you from time to time, giving your parents some respite to resuscitate themselves. Your grandmother has been an only child all her life, so was her mother, and a single mother too, raising her on her own. So they think girls are a good thing, in a way. Even if a whole slew of them were born, each would be unique. Well, unique...both unique and like them, extraordinary and identical, destined for the same fate as them and blessed with a wealth of other possibilities, who knows? Girls are the future of women, in their view. Girls are their future, but also their reflection. It keeps them going, both Grandma and Nana. They've had the vote for barely more than ten years, and they still don't always dare to exercise this right. But they have their hopes. They give you their mandate. You shall be unique, my granddaughter. But stay within the limits, all the same. Be polite. Be good. You never know.

Judging by the early photos of you, your parents resurface safely from the Styx, the ferry for the dead brings them back to the jetty. In this one, your mother's smiling gloriously at the camera—enough to make you wonder whether André took the picture. She's crouching and you're standing next to her, smiling, still looking somewhat Chinese, your eyes almonds lost in your cheeks.

You're wearing a little lace dress and white ankle socks, and your calves are sturdy. In this one you're in terry-cloth swimming briefs, standing to the right of your father who's in tight-fitting trunks, with your sister on his left, in briefs exactly like yours. The three of you are on a rock with a calm sea behind you. You and your sister both have very short hair, square shoulders, and no bikini tops, so that the pair of you with your father look like three strapping males at different stages of development. You're still chubby but less so: intrigued by your inflated appearance, your father eventually asked what you were being given for your afternoon snack every day and your grandmother replied, "Four bananas crushed with cream and sugar, why?" What business was it of her son-in-law's? Food isn't a man's concern. Girls have a sweet tooth, it's a recognized fact. Your father, meanwhile, doesn't want you to grow to the size of a cow. It's bad for the health and for finding a husband. Your family name may mean stacked but that doesn't give you free rein to turn into a beefcake. He stands up to the two old matrons and puts you on a banana-free diet (you're deeply indebted to him, he claims). You lose weight, but the nickname he gave you then will stay with you a long time: Big Belly. Your father's not one for subtlety. You're just a chubby girl, that's all. Meanwhile Claude, a little sparrow of a thing, will soon start calling you Fatta. Fatta as in Fat Ass. You're a candy-pink fat-ass big-belly combo (and candy-pink never made anyone look slimmer). But you don't check yourself out in the mirror yet, you're three years old.

You're three and you've already been going to school for six months: you wanted to go wherever it was your sister goes every day (jealous of the whiff of importance about her when she returns) and, because you've stopped wetting yourself, you're allowed in. Truth be told, for the first year you spend most of the time asleep, waking in a dormitory where all the other little beds are empty, looking like something from the fairy tales that people are starting to read to you. When you wake from your slumbers like Snow White surrounded by other beds, you don't remember your dreams or falling asleep. Your early childhood follows the same pattern: like a long sleep that you don't remember at all, except perhaps for a brief image, the occasional word. It is strange, though, almost worrying, knowing nothing about such a long period. Only witnesses can compensate for your amnesia, filling the void with their memories—which are distorted anyway, not to say contradictory—and a few photos whose black-and-white tones accentuate their age. What do they say? That you were the perfect baby, the perfect little girl, you slept well, you ate well ("Yes, that..." says your father), you hardly ever screamed, always smiled. The model child, they say. "Not a top model," your father adds, "hey, Big Belly?" "A little shy," your mother says. "At first, you'd be anxious with strangers, then sociable, and eventually downright inquisitive. Except you were...sulky, so sulky! At the sort of age when your sister was contrary, saying no to everything and stamping her foot, you didn't say anything, you sulked. Claude's always been a bit of a tomboy, stubborn, rebellious, a badass. From the age of two and a half, as soon as something didn't go your way, you'd slink off to a corner and sulk. A real girl, in other words! We sent you to school early because you were bored. You could already talk very well for your age."

And because you already speak well for your age and you're so interested in it all, in words, people, and the things people tell you, whether they're true or not; because three is the age for first recollections and you have a good memory; because from this point on you're self-aware, perhaps you can take over and tell this story yourself now. So what do you remember about being a girl?

2

My *first memory* begins with screaming, as if a nightmare
were waking me from the oblivion of sleep. The four of
us—my parents, my sister, Claude, and I—are together in
a hotel room in Le Lavandou, where the seaside photo
was taken. It's nighttime and I'm in a crib against a wall,
opposite the two beds, one double, one single. I wake to
the sound of my mother screaming, "Help! Someone came
in! There's a man in the room!" It starts with a word, like
the darkness. It is with this intrusion that I break into my
memory. My father gets out of bed, the door to the room
is open, there's scuffling from the end of the corridor. He
goes out but returns empty-handed, the man's vanished.
My mother's sitting up in bed, trying to calm her breathing, one fist balled against her naked breasts. It's very

hot and there are motionless ghosts at the windows. I'm shaking, I don't understand what's going on, did someone want to kill my mother? Or me? Could someone have hurt me? A man? "It was nothing," my father says, "just some rat stealing from hotel rooms. He didn't have time to take anything." A rat? And that's Daddy trying to reassure me! A rat that can get anywhere, like an insect, crawling like an ant into every hole and through the garbage? A rat with its long tail, so quick and elusive, a filthy, shameful thing poking its nose everywhere? Everyone goes back to sleep, except for me. I want to get into the big bed and sleep next to Mommy, I'm frightened he'll come back, but I daren't ask—Daddy wouldn't want me in their bed, anyway.

My second memory is from the following day, or perhaps the day before. My father's bought a blow-up boat with oars. He takes me off to Ali Baba's cave, which is quite a long way from the beach, he has to paddle for at least ten minutes. There's a crevice in the brown, seaweed-covered rocks, the thieves have hidden their treasure inside, and this is where they get in, you just have to say "Open sesame." I want to go looking for the treasure, but Daddy says no: what if the thieves were still there? It would be dangerous, and besides, that would be stealing too—yes you can rob a robber. So no entry, then. We go there several times in the boat, but we never see the treasure. The dinghy pitches beside the cleft rock, I peer into the depths with all my might, desperately searching for glints of gold, but it's very dark and I can't see a thing.

My father takes my sister and me to see it one after the other, never together. If the boat should capsize or suddenly deflate, even with our water wings on we could drown, and he wouldn't be able to save both of us, he'd have to choose. Now that's a father who thinks of everything, even death. Perhaps he's thinking of Gaëlle: girls do that, they die. Perhaps if one of the two of us had been a boy, he'd have taken us both in the boat. A boy's good and strong, a boy can always cope. But more tellingly, I think to myself, if one of us were a boy, he wouldn't hesitate if the boat went down, he'd know who to save.

The hotel is called Le Bathyscaphe. In the lobby, the owners exhibit a model of one of these submersibles along with a convoluted diagram of how it was assembled, and my father stands looking at it for ages—although I have no idea why. A bathyscaphe, he explains, pointing to the thing, is for going very, very deep under water. In one of these, people see the most wonderful things that you don't find anywhere else on earth. It's obvious he's longing to go down in one. The portholes look like the bulging eyes of a dead fish. The word itself is complicated. It means "deep vessel," I have trouble pronouncing it, ba-thy-sca-phe, but I've never forgotten it. Bathyscaphes are all the rage in the early '60s, people take an interest in their depth records; the deep-sea explorations of the *Trieste* and the *Archimedes* fascinate my father, who read all of Jules Verne as a boy. He's the one who tells me my first stories: the *Nautilus* and Ali Baba, the summer that I was three. I pretend to be thrilled by these tales of octopuses and periscopes, and my sister does too, but perhaps it's genuine in her case. Apart from the voice that's telling the stories, what is there to like? There's something missing from them if they're to capture my imagination. I'm not sure what. Girls, perhaps. There are no girls in these stories. We don't exist in his enthusiasm for passing them on. We're not there. It's only to be expected: Why on earth would a girl be twenty thousand leagues under the sea surrounded by danger and machines? But also, why are boys so keen on stories without girls in them?

I've asked my mother and my sister what they remember of that summer in Le Lavandou all those years ago. I thought that, even though—unlike me—it wasn't their first memory on this earth, they'd have clear recollections of our only vacation together. Because the four of us never went away anywhere again. Well, the only things my mother remembers are a trip in a paddleboat and the fact that I, Big Belly, would head off with my navel sticking out and go licking other people's ice creams when I'd finished my own. I was so cute no one could resist me, she says. As for my sister, she has absolutely no recollection of the hotel "rat" either, and when I tell her about it, she jeers: our parents were probably having sex, that's all; I've cooked up this whole scene from a few cries; I tinkered around with my opening scene and made it a crime, a sex crime.

That's certainly possible. Perhaps I needed to witness a scene from which I myself was excluded, to fill the memory gap that gave birth to me. The fear of that break-in is still undiminished, all these years later, tattooed into my body; it pierces my ears, just as my eyes can still see the entrance to the impenetrable sea cave, the one with the secret treasure. One day five years ago, I went back to Le Lavandou with Pierre, a crazy guy I was crazy about. We searched the beach in vain: there was no hotel called Le Bathyscaphe. Neither could I work out which rocks might have housed the Ali Baba cave. There are no cliffs at Le Lavandou. Did I invent it all? A dinghy gliding over the surface of things or a submarine exploring the depths, my memories or my imagination are taking me for a ride. "You started telling yourself stories when you were three," Pierre concluded, slicing into the sand with a razor clam. "You were precocious, as a girl."

I'm precocious, as a girl, or rather, I'm precocious, like a girl: I'm better at talking than walking, better at listening than running, I'd rather play with words than play off-ground tag. Apparently, language is our privilege, those of us who learn at such an early age to limit our bodies. Words are our *Nautilus*, they have their hidden depths.

At nursery school, when I'm not sleeping I look every-where for my sister, but she doesn't factor me in, she's whispering away with other big girls who giggle when they look over at me, and she very soon changes schools, going to the one across the street. I don't see her till the end of the day when she scowls to acknowledge that I'm still alive—and chatty with it too, nattering on about my day—and is also irritated to find me dressed like her, a fake twin with chubby cheeks, when she's always dreamed of being unique, the only one...and what about me, then! Being an only child, like my friend Jeannine, that must be wonderful! Claude and I do often wear the same clothes, as if everything comes in packs of two in Rouen. In fact, they're made from the same fabric remnant, and Nana, who was once a seamstress, makes two skirts or two Sunday-best dresses with flowers or smocking or pink bows. It's economical having two girls. Otherwise there'd have to be another design: boys need a different pattern, they're made of other material. On the way home from school, Claude walks ahead of me, swinging her shoul-ders, whistling between her fingers, behaving as if I wasn't there, and when I complain because I can't keep up she calls me a sissy. I can see what Claude wants. Her vocation is to be an only son.

On the subject of boys, it has to be said that, apart from in Daddy's stories and obliquely in Mommy's con-versations, there aren't many of them around in the early days. Our cousins are not yet born, our neighbors have retired, and our parents don't spend much time with friends, particularly if they have boys. At nursery school, even though there's only one building, the classes are not mixed. The schoolyard is communal, but we use it at different times. There are just a few activities that bring us together, such as the distribution of dreary glasses of milk in the morning, and occasional puppet shows when a few of the boys shout so loudly to warn Guignol that Gnafron's lying in wait for him that it makes some of the girls cry. There's no need because if you move a little to the side you can see the two teachers—both of them girls—wielding the puppets and putting on deep voices. Observation 1: girls are very good at being boys, when they want to. There are also sessions when we learn folk dances from other countries and regions; something that, according to the High Commission for Youth and Sports, promotes mixed-sex friendships and motor skills. These sessions are opportunities to settle the enigma: What *is* a boy? And its corrosive corollary: Is a boy better? This question, not that it bothers me much (the answer is no), rears its head every now and then. The first time that it occurs to me, it's thanks to the layout of the premises: Our classrooms and segregated play areas are separated by the girls' restrooms and the boys' restrooms. The figure on the boys' door has two legs. The one for the girls wears a skirt. Obviously (but why?), we're not allowed to go into the boys' restroom, and yet you need only walk past for the difference to jump out at you through the half-open door: It's painted blue. Plus, there's a row of tiny handbasins set low on the wall and the boys pee into them, well, they try—sometimes one of the teachers helps them, or she scolds them. Observation 2: boys are different, they pee standing up. Okay, I already knew that, I've seen Daddy get out of the car more than once to go and commune with a tree trunk like he wanted to tell it a secret. He can do this anywhere he likes along the road, but for us, for girls, it's a whole performance; when I squat, ants and policemen start trying to clamber all over me, I wish I could hold on but often I can't and we have to stop the car (girls are such pee-ers, my father says). On the other hand, generalizing is pointless. Take my friend Thérèse. She lives on the farm opposite our house in La Chaux in the Auvergne, where my grandfather was born. My sister and I spend all of our summer vacations in La Chaux with our grandparents. Despite Grandma's protests, we go over every day to help Thérèse do her dishes—she has three boys and a cantankerous husband, none of whom ever get up from the table, I've noticed. They work in the cowshed or the fields while she goes up to Huit-Fons with her cows. There's Periwinkle, Daisy, Cutie, Duchess, and Mirabelle, they all have girls' names—of course they do, they're mommies, they make milk. Thérèse teaches us to recognize each one and call to them in the local patois to round them up. It's wonderful when they obey, when their great bulk moves just at the sound of our voices, we feel powerful. Claude and I go up the mountain with her to look for green grass, even though I struggle because it's a steep climb. "Come on, Fatta, put your back into it," my sister says. Well, Thérèse sometimes slows down on those rocky paths, picks up her layers of petticoats, and pees standing up, hardly even spreading her legs. Balto the dog lifts his leg; not her. It spouts straight out, like a cow's, making the same sound as it streams over the stones. Thérèse doesn't even stop talking and then just sets off again. What really thrills my sister and me is that, you see, it's obvious she's not wearing panties. And she doesn't hide herself either, she's not ashamed, no more than the cows who drop their dung without even slowing down. "That's country girls for you," my grandmother says, "they do it like animals." Or, as per Observation 1, they do it like boys, if they want to. Well, when they can. Thérèse made me try one time, it went all over my socks. Not easy for a city girl. Having said that, whether you're in the city or the country, boys get help in this procedure from a little length of tube resting on a floppy cushion; they use it to do their watering left, right, and center without any warning. The birth of our cousin Bruno the year I turned four confirms my intuition. He has a tube that I don't have, neither does Claude, nor my dolls, nor Sophie the giraffe, nor Mommy under her fur when she takes a bath with us, and not even

Teddy, my cuddly bear. A tiny little blip of a thing that my aunt cleans as carefully as she does the crystal drops on the chandelier in the living room, referring to it adoringly as "my little bird"—*my*, when she doesn't have one herself, that's just the point, hers must have flown away. Observation 3, Revelation 1: that's the whole thing. *Their* thing. It doesn't look like much, but it's quite a thing. If there's nothing, it's a girl. Girls have nothing.

On the other hand, well, what good is it to them, what's it *for*, apart from staying standing instead of sitting down in a stall? Is it better? I'd say it's less practical, actually, apart from outdoors. Not so comfortable. Still, I do some experimenting with the hose in the vegetable garden, wedging it between my legs and pointing it toward the potatoes or the tomatoes, I sprinkle it over my sister who tries and fails to grab it from me. Basically, I do whatever I like with it and I have to admit it's fun. Apart from that, I feel good around girls at school, we're the same. We play together and sing, they're careful to slip out of the dormitory quietly so as not to wake me—the girls in my class are kind. There are one or two who pull my hair, but their mommies come to apologize, and they don't do it again. Life is nice, for a girl, which rhymes with unfurl— the days unfurl gently, sweetly . . . well, life is nice at school at least (at home it's another story). I don't think about boys unless I see one, but then I really do think about them, I put my mind to it. Between the ages of three and six, while I'm at the Jeanne d'Arc Nursery School, I hone my knowledge. The folk-dancing days are particularly useful. We're put in pairs, a girl and a boy, like parents, like grown-ups. It's an opportunity to touch a boy, talk to one, understand what it is. I very soon have a devoted partner and take to dancing with him alone. He's called Jacques, he's five years old, and he has one hand missing. Just like a nursery rhyme I remember from those early days: "*My little bird, did you hurt yourself? Did you hurt, on the wing, did you hurt, on the wing, did you hurt yourself?*" To be more precise, one of his hands is made of pale yellow plastic and feels the same as my doll Bella, which makes him seem familiar. Anyway, he's not as screwy as the other boys and concentrates on his steps. I like his weakness, it makes me strong. He may be missing a hand, but I have two, I can help him. This boy has something to be sad about, and I'm going to make him forget it. "*My little bird, do you want to make it better? Do you want, on the wing, do you want, on the wing, do you want to make it better?*" We really do look great, even though we dance in slippers and his hand can't steer mine. I'm the one steering him. I lead the dance, I'm lead partner. Observation 1: girls are very good at being boys, when they want to be. Jacques is glad that I'm not squeamish about holding his lifeless hand. He smiles at me and at the end of the day he runs out to introduce me to his mommy. Observation 4: girls can make things better for boys, if they—the boys—want it. "*I want to make it better and to marry you, and to ma-, on the wing, and to ma-, on the wing, and to marry you.*" "Is he your boyfriend?" my mother asks. "He has beautiful eyes." His eyes are the same blue as André's, that's why she says that.

The other opportunity to study boys is in the park outside school where I go to play with my best friend Jeannine. Apart from a slide and a two-seater swing, there's not much fun to be had there. We often find the same two boys on this swing, spreading their arms like the wings of planes, never leaving this chosen flight path—they're so annoying. One day I get an idea: We wrap some smooth round pebbles in candy wrappers and offer them in exchange for a ride on the swing. The boys hesitate for a moment, suspecting a trap, then eventually accept and surrender the swing to us. They're not happy when they find the pebbles, but Jeannine and I couldn't give a damn. The best bit is what happens next, when we really...get into the swing of it. A few days later we find the same boys on the swing and we offer them candy. Oh no, they're not falling for that again, they say, they know what we're like! But we swear we're not tricking them this time, we're sorry about the other day, honestly, this time the candy's real, and to prove it we eat one in front of them, come on, let's make up. They look at each other, reach a silent agreement, and slip off the swing, and Jeannine and I jump straight onto it. "We knew it..." they say when they see that it's pebbles again, but we're laughing so hard we don't hear them. Observation 5: their thing doesn't make them any cleverer than girls—in fact, it's the opposite. Still, this is only a provisional conclusion. Deep down, I can't believe boys are as stupid as all that. Isn't it more that they want to be kind, but they don't want anyone to know? They let us manipulate them, they agree to look like suckers and would rather play along with our trick than admit that they want to please us. On the strength of that, I think, here's Observation 6: boys secretly want to please girls. So it's more complicated than it appears. To be investigated.

Another means of learning is to study parents, in other words a boy and a girl who've been living together since they became grown-ups. At first glance, it doesn't look like a barrel of laughs. I don't know much about Daddy apart from the fact that, except when he's making a joke, he doesn't smile a great deal—and never at Mommy. They sleep together, they eat together, they don't talk to each other, except about money or us—or some people who made some "landings," some English people, but we never see them. They don't have many friends, or only each his or her own. He doesn't seem to want to please her anymore. They never kiss like in *Snow White*, and never dance together. But what I'm really interested to know is whether Daddy has the same tiny little thing between his legs as our baby cousin does—it would be so ridiculous that I want to see it to believe it. On Sundays he always comes out of the shower with a towel around his hips and goes through the dining room to get to the bedroom, so my sister and I hide under the table and go into contortions trying to catch a glimpse of what he's hiding, but it doesn't work. Meanwhile, Mommy likes pretty dresses and makeup. She goes to the hair salon every Saturday morning, then in the afternoon she goes shopping with Grandma. They come home with parcels and try things on again in front of the mirror. Mommy often demolishes the lacquered helmet of her hair with a sweep of her hairbrush because the hairdresser didn't understand what she wanted at all. Then she paints her fingernails and chats with Grandma over a cup of tea, talking about dresses or about André. Mommy likes being up-to-date with fashion, she's slim and elegant, which doesn't stop her flicking her nose pickings under the armchairs. Grandma's the one who pays for the shopping because Daddy wouldn't agree to it; if I've got this right, he doesn't like unnecessary expenditure, dresses, perms, mascara, all that stuff. His father repaired watches and he may be a doctor, but he has the crummiest office in Rouen and a laughable turnover; in other words, they're not exactly born out of Croesus's thigh. Even when the things Mommy buys are for Claude and me, he's not happy: those pink dresses must have cost a fortune! They look like rich folks' kids in them!

Well, I think I look pretty in my dress, even if my sister does have the same one. I twirl in front of the mirror, like

Mommy. But maybe I'm wrong, seeing as Daddy doesn't like it?

One evening some men come by the house to ask some questions. They sit at the dining-room table with Daddy and one of them checks boxes on a form he's taken from his briefcase. By my calculations, this must be the 1964 census, I'm five years old. Shy but also inquisitive, I hide behind the sofa.

"Do you have any children?" asks one of the men.

"No," replies my father. "I have two daughters."

3

I can read at five, I learned along with my sister. The pictures scare me more than the words: I throw the book of *Snow White* on top of the wardrobe because the witch on the front cover terrifies me, but I read Hans Christian Andersen's tales again and again, even if they're often terribly sad. I like crying, though, and no one criticizes me for this—girls have a right to. I am by turns the little match girl whom nobody listens to, who dies unnoticed in the cold; the incredibly sensitive princess with the pea; and the little mermaid who has to sacrifice her voice to win her place alongside the prince, then has to sacrifice herself to save his life. My mother reads *Sleeping Beauty* to me when she has time. My favorite bit is when the princess wakes because the prince has kissed her and she says,

"You took your time." I think it's funny, chiding him like that, unabashed, a little imperious, as is fitting for a princess. She's right. I mean, he did take a hundred years to find her, prince or no prince, and even on a horse—that's a long time. But girls wait as long as they have to, they're patient if the reward is love. "*Someday my prince will come...to be happy forever, I know.*" It's my first trip to the movies. The song in *Snow White* is a promise, and a promise is something that's kept. The kiss always comes eventually, you just have to wait. Fine, there are some girls who head off in search of it, who don't sit at home in their slippers, especially not glass ones. Little Gerda, for example, she sets off barefoot into the huge world to bring home her friend Kay who's being held prisoner by the Snow Queen. She gets so tired and tackles so many obstacles that a whole eternity has elapsed when they finally find each other. "The old clock went tick-tock, the hands pointed to the time of day, but as they came through the doorway, they realized they had become grown-ups." I know the end by heart and when Mommy reads it, I always say the closing sentences along with her. I like the sense of time that they conjure, the future that they anticipate, but oh, life seems so long, and love so far away! Should I be setting out already? Is it up to girls to forge ahead? No, they must wait instead, like Mommy when she hovers behind the curtains keeping an eye out for André: he's on his way, then all of a sudden, he's there and a hundred years are gone in flash.

Claude meanwhile isn't very keen on fairy tales. She says I'm a baby. In our grandparents' apartment, which is an extension of our own, she shuts herself in the office with Corinne, a cousin whom Daddy has nicknamed Pigtail because she always has pigtails, and she doesn't have a big belly. They try to keep me out, but I go in anyway. They haul big volumes of the *Quillet* encyclopedia from the bookshelves and look for dirty words: pecker, wiener, and johnson for boys; itty-bit for girls. Not one of them is in the dictionary, serves them right! Only "thingy" appears as: "A person or thing that the speaker cannot or does not wish to name." Well, that speaks volumes! As for itty-bit, no one but my sister and me knows the word. When I mention it to Jeannine, she shrugs and says, "You mean a puffpuff?" "Foofoo," Corinne corrects her. "Your lady bits," says Ginette. "A mini moo." It's like no two people have the same word to describe the thing, or the absence of a thing. Later, when I've seen the word "sex" on a form that my father left on the living-room table—he'd checked "male," above "female"—I do my own research in the dictionary. The word "sex," I discover, is related to the Latin *secare*, which means "to cut" and has spawned, among others, the verbs "section" and "bisect," and the word "secateurs." Aha, I'm starting to understand: boys' pee-pees are sex-tioned off to turn them into girls. But where and when? It must be hideously painful, it must bleed more than a knee when you fall off your bike, even if there is only a small scar left behind, a narrow cleft between the thighs, but try as I might, I don't remember it. And what about the ones who got to keep the thing, why them? Who chose? Definitely not my father, in any event. A girl is an injured boy. Rather like Jacques when he unscrews his plastic hand. And what are they being punished for, these boys made into girls? I can't answer that, it's beyond me. I don't remember ever being a boy, but somewhere deep inside me I'm not surprised. I feel like a boy, sometimes. Not exactly the same, but not different, apart from pink and dresses. They show off, move around a lot, and laugh loudly. But look at me, I can do everything a boy can, apart from pee standing up (and even that...). It's just I don't want to.

I read whenever I have a moment to myself, and I have plenty. My mind brims with stories and I tell them to my doll. My favorite is *The Little Princess*. It's about Sara, a very pretty, very intelligent little girl growing up in an expensive girls' boarding school, but when her father dies, she becomes a poor orphan. Thrown out by the school where she was once the star pupil, she ends up living in a garret and begging for food until the day when her little room under the eaves starts filling with beautiful furniture and delicious food while a warming fire blazes in the grate. She doesn't understand thanks to whom all these wonders are happening or how—through the window, from the roof?—and I don't understand it either. It transpires—as we find out at the end—that she has a benefactor: a man, of course. At night I have little-princess dreams. Or rather I always have the same dream, I start it when I'm wide awake and then start it over in my sleep. I live in a comfortable house—not a castle, I'm a commoner princess—and every time I open a cupboard, a closet, or the fridge to take something out, the thing is immediately replaced by another one that's more beautiful, more succulent, and more exactly what I want. Every night I pirouette in new dresses, eat meringues and candy, and wear patent leather shoes. That dream is with me all through my early childhood, banishing anxieties: nothing is missing, I have everything I need.

When I'm not at school I'm very often at my grandmother's, I just have to walk through one door. She always stays at home in the morning, unlike her mother, my great-grandmother, who heads off *to the shop* every morning. She arrives at her perfumery at nine o'clock, she's the boss and has two employees, one of whom, Renée, she sometimes invites to Sunday lunch. Nana's hair is completely white with a purplish gleam. No one thinks it strange that of all the girls in the house spread across four generations, it's the eldest who works, the only one to earn any money. My father doesn't like Nana very much, or maybe Nana doesn't like him very much, I don't know, but still, he often cites her as a good example at mealtimes, he sometimes even makes Mom cry, especially when she has a new lipstick. He tells Claude and me that we absolutely must have a trade, like Nana. It could be hairdressing, teaching, nursing, whatever we like but it matters: we mustn't go on thinking we'll be twiddling our thumbs all day—he gives Mom a sideways glance—we're not daddy's girls. Mom *is* then, if I've understood that right. Her father, Grandpa Maurice, gave her the apartment and the car, and even bought my father's doctor's office to add to her wedding gifts—he took the smallest one in Rouen with no patients as yet, but all the same... It's called a dowry. I learn the word from Grandma and will come across it later in Molière's plays: money given to a girl to make it easier for her to find a husband. "But then how do you know if it's love or just for the money?" I ask. "It doesn't have to be one or the other," Grandma replies. Mom is a daddy's girl, like in fairy tales where fathers are kings. When Claude and I are married, we won't have anything at all; that's the difference. We'll be nobody's girls. Without dowries. We don't know what job Prince Charming will have, but he won't choose the little minx who sleeps while she waits for him to show up. Sleeping beauty, claptrap! Never heard of her. Fatta won't have a magic, self-stocking fridge. Understood? Understood. Promise? Promise. On the other hand, Daddy's actually doing very well out of the money that's given to girls, so it's not very logical. He often says, "Money doesn't make you happy but it helps." He doesn't seem happy, though. We, meanwhile, will be loved for who we are when we're grown-ups. Or perhaps we'll never be loved? I'm tormented by these thoughts: how will I cope without money *or* love? Luckily, there are dreams. And anyway, what does Daddy know about our future, shut away in that *Nautilus*?

My grandfather is never at home either (he has a factory that makes plastic and gobbles time, and he runs the rugby club), so the house belongs to us girls. My grandmother has a very strict daily routine. After breakfast every day she does the housework, going from one room to the next with her feather duster and her orange cloth. She could have a maid but then what would she do all morning? I admire her punctiliousness, finding its regularity as fascinating as it is scary: Will I have to do the same when I'm a grown-up? Going over the same tasks ad infinitum, endlessly repeating myself while life goes on outside? My grandmother's routine is comforting, she knows what she has to do and sees the results—and so do I: everything is as clean and tidy as if it's been replaced, brand-new every day. She hunts down the dust that we all turn into—the preacher read about it in Bible study: "You are dust and you shall return to dust." No one can avoid it, he said, but my grandmother's trying. She sweeps aside death with a flick of her hand, picking off all the corpses that collect on top of wardrobes. She keeps life going. On the other hand, I realize anxiously, it will all stop when she dies. Who will keep up her impossible task? I don't want to take on the mantle. Besides, she never asks me to help her, she doesn't teach me how to do the housework. Princesses have a different destiny, in the outside world, like men. So I trail after her, telling her stories, and she enjoys it, although she sometimes says I'm definitely a girl, *a real chatterbox.* When I've had enough, I go back through the connecting door and rejoin Mom. She does housework too, but not so much, she doesn't go into the corners, she's twenty-eight, real life is going on somewhere else. She starts making a blanquette or an apple pie, she often stops at eleven for a slice of *saucisson* and a glass of wine—a little hit of red, she calls it. She waits for André to call between viewings—he's a realtor. He calls from clients' houses so his wife doesn't hear him, she explains to Grandma who comes to join her when she's cleaned herself up. It's a bit frustrating, she says, because he can't talk about love. Then she puts records on the turntable, even though Daddy doesn't like anyone using it when he's out, he says it'll get broken. She dances the twist to Petula Clark and coaxes Claude and me to join her, while Grandma sits on the edge of a pink armchair, watching us indulgently, or happily, or perhaps wanting to join us—she's only forty-eight, after all. Mommy also listens to Sacha Distel and Richard Anthony, "*How can I live in a world without you, I love you more than you know, I love you, and I'll never live without you,*" and that's when she usually starts talking about André and Daddy again, she says horrible things, referring to him as Matthieu: Matthieu's a cheapskate, Matthieu never talks to her, Matthieu's good for noth— Sometimes Grandma glares at her, not in front of the girls, but Mom keeps going, she must think we don't know Daddy's called Matthieu, she must think we're a bit dumb. There's also a song I hate. The refrain goes: "*Would you mind, sir, if I borrowed your daughter?*" I think the lyrics are stupid, you can't borrow a girl like borrowing a book from the library because a girl isn't a thing, plus a girl isn't something you give back, you keep her—at least, that's what happens in fairy tales. The singer's called Adamo, which is Adam in Italian. Well, I'll have you know, the first man seems like an idiot.

When I'm not reading, I play with my doll. I take her stroller around all the rooms. Bella is blond with blue eyes, there's a real family likeness between us. Her birthday's the same day as mine, and I always give her a dress or a hair clip for her curly hair. One time, my parents take us on a visit to Andrè and his wife who have two children about the same age as we are, Mom tells us—"a boy and a girl," she adds a little wistfully. I take Bella with me. Christiane is ten, the same age as Claude, and Gilbert is younger than I am, he still needs help going to the bathroom— the four of us go together, all three girls giggling, and he blushes bright red. There's a toy garage with an elevator for the cars and a spiraling ramp. He doesn't really like it when we send his green Simca 1000 hurtling down, but Claude does it every time. Christiane has much prettier dolls than mine, they talk and move their arms—there's even one that pees if you give her a bottle of water. The strange thing is that Christiane's not allowed to have her dolls the whole time. She has to ask permission from her mother, who says yes or no. If she says yes (which she usually does when we're there), she opens the door to a wardrobe using a big key, and inside it's Christmas: amazing dolls standing in a line on the shelves; and other, smaller ones in a house with lovely furniture, pink mirrors, vases, hairbrushes, and jewelry, rather like in my dream. Christiane's mother takes out a doll, just one at a time, and we're allowed to play with her for an hour or two, then she goes back into the closet. Christiane is sad but her mother is unrelenting, "they mustn't get spoiled." As for Gilbert, he has his ball, his cars, his LEGO set, and even a tricycle, all readily available in his bedroom, because "they're more robust." Girls are like dolls—fragile in their calf-length dresses, and they mustn't get dirty. And there's another thing I've noticed: when Gilbert farts his parents laugh, but if one of us does, they tell us it's dirty and we should restrain ourselves. Girls show every speck of dirt. We now visit André and his wife nearly every weekend. Their house is out in the country, fifteen minutes from Rouen. When Christiane's dolls are locked away, we take mine for walks and she smiles at her good luck, or we play shop using pots of jam made with mirabelle plums from the garden. Gilbert sometimes plays the customer, paying us in Monopoly money which he produces in great wads. One Sunday before the vacation I forget Bella in Christiane's bedroom. I snivel in the back of the car but Daddy refuses to turn around to get her, I'll have her back soon enough, two weeks'll go by quickly. Next time we're there, I immediately hunt through every room for Bella. I can't find her. Christiane's mom must have put her away in the closet with the others. "No," she says coolly. She gave her to the Catholic charity, they need toys for the poor. We must all learn to share. Mommy doesn't say anything, she looks over at André. Daddy looks annoyed, to make things worse he's a Protestant, but he doesn't say anything either. "Why didn't she donate Gilbert's toys instead?" Claude asks. Oh, how I love my sister sometimes! Christiane's wicked mother turns to me with a, "Well, you should have taken better care of your doll. You abandoned her. It's your own fault."

In the car on the way home I cry so much that Mommy says, "Come on, stop crying. We'll buy you another one." "Buying, always buying," Dad snaps. "Sylvie's right—our girls aren't good at sharing." Mom doesn't reply, she's had more than enough of sharing André. I cry all the louder, I don't want another doll, it's Bella that I want. Years later I'll still remember those words and that tearful little girl in the backseat of the car, the child whose dolly was taken. When you're seven—or at any age—it's not learning to share something that's difficult. It's learning to lose something. It seems girls are forced into this thankless task much earlier, they have to tackle it more frequently and they cope with it less well. Sadness beckons them. Maybe they refuse to be cornered into defeat. Maybe we refuse to accept it's a losing battle, even when we know it is.

There's no school on Thursdays and Mom doesn't really want to take us to the tennis club with her. I know that before the little princess became an orphan, she had dancing classes, so Mom enrolls us in Martinet's classes, considered the best in Rouen. The lessons are hard, we have to repeat the same moves and correct our positions again and again. "Fourth, I said fourth," the teacher enunciates, with his cane in his hand, condemning an arm with not quite the right curve, an in-turned foot or a too-straight knee. I'm graceful and I carry myself well, parading with the gravity of a pope with an illustrated *Larousse* dictionary on my head, my eyes locked onto their reflection in the mirror, my chin unmoving, "un-mo-ving," Mr. Martinet says. I'm cultivating a princess's deportment which will mostly entitle me to being called a stuck-up little madam in the schoolyard. Claude, on the other hand, is more physical, she can do the crab and turn cartwheels, and she laughs when I collapse on the floor, dragged down by the weight of my great belly. "Claude is supple and Laurence is graceful," Mr. Martinet explains to my grandmother, hoping to give us an introduction to the ballet company at Opéra de Paris. "Between the two of you, you'd make a perfect star ballerina," my grandfather jokes when the compliment is relayed to him. The Opéra de Paris? I dream of going there, but not with my sister, just with my mother and grandmother. Well, I dream about it but I'm also frightened. Dad doesn't want us to have a television, but at my grandparents' house I've secretly managed to watch almost every episode of *L'Âge heureux*. It's a series about child ballet students at the Opéra; it ends well but the girls are so horrible to each other, jealous and everything! There's one who'll stoop to the worst tricks to secure the lead role. That's pretty much the premise of every story about girls, in fact, when you come to think of it, not to mention stories about sisters. There's always a witch in their midst, or one sister who spews out snakes.

On the subject of stories, Nana has worked out that when her son-in-law, my grandpa Maurice, comes home very late, it's not only because he's been talking to his accountant or bawling out his scrum half. She'd made her little inquiries so she eventually told Grandma: it's because of a big blond woman who sometimes comes to buy rice powder from her shop. She spotted Grandpa Maurice having dinner with her in the brasserie near the train station, then they left together in his car. Apparently, the woman's hoping to get herself set up with a bar-cum-tobacconist, which is why Nana decided to tip off her daughter. Grandma's voice sounds different when she asks, "Is she pretty? How old is she? Is she single? Do you think he loves her?" Nana says the woman's coarse with her straw-colored hair and she's only after Maurice's money. "She's a hussy, a slut, a floozy"—Nana produces a succession of words I don't know, I'll go and look them up in the dictionary as soon as I can sneak out unnoticed from behind the sofa where I'm hiding with my Barbie—"a harlot, a strumpet, a trollop, scum of the earth," and when Grandma keeps sniveling, apparently unsure whether the threat is serious, whether her husband is going to ask for a divorce, Nana shrugs and concludes, "Oh, come on, what are you fussing about? I mean, I told you, she's a girl."

The girls at Martinet's are mostly kind, even if they do beg for compliments and smile at their reflections in the mirror as they strike their poses. It has to be said, I do the same because I'm obsessed with my pale pink tutu, the tulle is so dainty, like a fairy's hat, and the satin on my demi-pointes is so soft (my Barbie has the same outfit but she's much prettier than I am, without even a hint of a belly). And then there's Julien. He's the only boy and the moms who stay to watch the classes give him funny looks. He's shy and all skinny in his leotard and gray tights from which a tiny outline protrudes . . . Mr. Martinet sometimes calls it his semicolon—yet another name for their thingy, I notice. "Protect your semicolon, Julien!" he barks when we raise a leg, and he laughs a terrifying laugh. It's nothing like the huge mounds on display between the dancers' legs at the adult group's end-of-year show. Claude and I are paralyzed by the sight of them, but by all accounts it's not their thingies, not for real, just a casing to protect their thingies. Girls, on the other hand, have nothing—nothing to protect, apparently. Their breasts are mounds too, but don't seem to be so vulnerable—they protect them with bras. Claude and I can't wait to have bras ourselves, even if there is metal in them, what Nana calls "boning," we've no idea why. Julien doesn't do exactly the same exercises as us; the teacher explains that in classical ballet the boy is there to carry the girl, to support her, showcase her, "just like in life," he says, turning his grinning face toward the mothers. They smile. I personally don't really get how this little pip-squeak Julien could carry a fat ass like me but we'll have to see. My stomach sticks out and my back is too arched, so Mom takes me to see a doctor then a physiotherapist (I hear "fizzy O therapist" and wonder if I'll be offered an orange soda), but Mr. Martinet can't see the problem: what's seen as graceful in dance is called lordosis by science. "An arched back in a ballerina is very good," he says, appraising my behind. One day during the Easter vacation, when Claude and I are waiting by the bus that will take us to our vacation camp, I see Julien crying and clinging to his mother, wailing that he doesn't want to go. The other kids laugh at him whining like a girl, but not me, first, because I *am* a girl, second, because I'm doing exactly the same as Julien—howling, calling my mother, begging her to keep me at home—but all internally, my distress kept hidden inside so no one sees it; Julien is acting out in public the scene that's going on inside my body, invisibly, secretly. I know (I've already tried) that all it will achieve is to irritate Mommy who can't wait for the bus to carry us away for two weeks—two wonderful weeks without us, two long weeks without her. One of the instructors hoists Julien onto the bus almost by force; Julien struggles then squishes his nose against the window so that his tears stream down it. I admire him for having the courage that I lack, the courage to show his feelings, but at the same time I look down on him, I'm not sure which it is. His crying distracts me from my own thanks to the question that it poses on the subject of boys: So, are they sensitive, then, despite what people say? Could there be boys who value love more highly than their pride in being boys? I'm so plagued by these questions that when we're home from camp I describe the tearful scene over lunch, and I'm allowed to because Daddy's progressive, he thinks it only natural that children should speak at the table. Now, he must know a thing or two about boys. Mommy had noticed Julien crying on the day we left, she remembers it very clearly, "Ah, boys and their mothers," she sighs, "it's quite something..." She's not in any position to know but she's obviously imagining it. "And he takes dance classes with you?" my father asks casually while he peels an orange. "Well, that one'll grow up gay..." I'm across from him and I sit there wide-eyed. Gay? How can such a tearful little boy end up happy? "I mean, I'd say there are all the ingredients for a future queen..." A queen? Where does royalty come into it? "No, a queen just means someone effeminate." Effeminate? I'm hungry for new vocabulary. "Effeminate means someone who behaves like a woman," explains my father, always happy to teach me something new. I nod to show that I understand that "like a woman" is not a positive characteristic. After that I don't have much time to study Julien's behavior in more detail, or to compare it to any queens around the world. Because when Claude is showering one day Mom notices the big red wheals on her thighs. They're from the cane that the aptly named Mr. Martinet uses and abuses on the stubborn, rebellious Claude when she disobeys his instructions. Mom's not really sure whether that's normal (you have to suffer to be beautiful) or this physical abuse goes beyond a teacher's privileges. What does Matthieu think? Matthieu thinks the blanquette is too salty and we should stop dancing straightaway, the man's a sadistic pervert. If you ask me, what Matthieu's most concerned about is that his daughters shouldn't turn into queens. Dancing is effeminate. So's playing the piano, it must be, because he doesn't want me to learn that either. There was a concert at school and I came home afterward buzzing with emotion, eager to be able to play like the man; he closed his eyes at some points, shaking his curly hair, he seemed to be carried away by the music—he was a queen too, no doubt about it. And yet Daddy often listens to that sort of music in the evenings, after we've gone to bed. Piano music, or organ, sad stuff. Well okay, it's not the same, Daddy's not a queen. When he's not listening to music, he reads detective books with pictures of girls in swimsuits with targets on their stomachs. The books have funny titles like *Straw Poll in Panama*, *Rumpus in Zanzibar*, and *The Bulgarian Panther Woman*. He sometimes passes them on to my grandfather. Grandpa's not effeminate either. When he was young he played on the French national rugby team and even played international matches. The photos show him hunkered down next to the oval ball, he has beautiful fine hands, not like the props who have huge thighs and jaws like animals, but I don't say so. He now runs the club in Rouen. When the Five Nations Championship is on television, he shuts himself in the living room with ten other former players. My grandmother gingerly takes in a tray laden with beers and scuttles straight back out. At regular intervals we hear roaring from the smoke-filled room—furious protests, cheers of joy, or groans; through the frosted glass in the door I can see shadows suddenly slumping, leaping up from chairs, or raising their arms and knocking back their bottles of beer. Sometimes glass gets broken, the carpet will be stained, and Nana grumbles snidely from the far end of the kitchen. I stay in the corridor, banished. "Whatever you do, don't go in," my grandmother tells me. I have absolutely no desire to.

In any event, my artistic career is curtailed when I'm eight: no dancing or piano, but I'm still allowed to read. Not comic books, though, except *Asterix* for the Latin, *Lucky Luke* because cowboys aren't queens, and *Tintin* which is already a classic—come to think of it, he has something of a queen about him, but then there's Captain Haddock who drinks a lot of whiskey, and that's definitely manly. For her part, Claude couldn't care less about stopping dancing, she prefers theater. At Christmas she orders a costume for her favorite TV character, Thierry la Fronde, and I get an Isabelle outfit; she orchestrates episodes for the two of us, in which she saves my skin in the nick of time and haughtily allows me to kiss her cheek while she adjusts my wig with the blond braids on top of my actual blond braids. The lead actor, Jean-Claude Drouot, is handsome in his tights, and so is my sister, even though in her case there's nothing between her legs. Sometimes, just to annoy her, I sing: "*Thierry la Fronde is a total loser, Thierry la Fronde is a waste of space, his slingshot's plastic anyway, it came from a dime store by the way.*" When I'm all alone at home I wistfully put on my pink dancing tights and try out a few steps in front of the mirror. I'll never be a star dancer. Still, my taste for dance is dented by the school show that we perform at the end of second grade. As stipulated by the headmistress's staging, some girls are made to look like flowers in dresses with pink corollas, others, including Jeannine and myself, have butterfly costumes. If I'd had the choice, I'd have preferred to be a flower, they're prettier and they don't move so much, they unfurl in the morning sun in their petal costumes; but I'm actually quite proud of mine which is bright and multicolored—Nana made it out of shop-display satin, the only thing made by the teacher are the wire antennae attached to my head. So we flit around the roses in the covered playground, tilting toward them and then fluttering away again in front of all the parents and every child in the school. All at once, my antennae become tangled with Jeannine's, we struggle and heave to break apart but it's no good, we're no longer butterflies but goats, while the choreography continues around us. In the end, the teacher hauls us off the stage and leaves us to sort ourselves out, watched by smiling parents and sniggering boys in the front row. I'm paralyzed with shame; humiliation is a revelation, it's all-consuming. The boys laugh and I feel like a nothing. It doesn't last long, but it will come back. Sniggering boys appear in my dreams. There I am with them watching me, and I'm watching me from outside myself, I watch the little girl struggling with no one to help her, her head lowered as she flaps her wings, I watch her struggling in her trap, failing to free herself, twice, three times, then slowing in her attempts, then giving up. Is that the fate that girls and butterflies have in common?

4

I can see her, I say. Across the intervening years, I see myself in that child as if looking in a mirror, but it's someone else that "things" happen to, otherwise I can't do it. She comes out of the rabbit shed where she just slipped some carrot tops through the wire netting of the hutch. She's wearing gingham shorts and a pink blouse. I don't know exactly how old she is, I'd say rising nine: it's the first summer at La Chaux without her grandpa Maurice, and this couldn't have happened before, when he was alive, no one would have dared. It didn't happen later either because the year she turned ten she was ill the whole time, that was the year that her skin complained, that her whole body lodged complaints.

The man is her grandfather's older brother, his name is Félix and, like her mother, she calls him Unky. She only ever sees him during the summer vacation at La Chaux when everyone comes together, young or old: it's the "family seat," they say, and she always pictures them all—with her in the middle—squished into an armchair like her dolls. She doesn't much like this uncle, there's something odd about him. But he comes to play cards in the evenings; snuggled in her bed, she hears them late into the night, the grown-ups, laughing and shouting under the kitchen light. She can see them through a crack where the doorframe doesn't join properly. When her mother is there she always wins, she's good at cards. And Félix brings them zucchinis and lettuce from his vegetable garden.

He's actually beckoning her over to the lettuce right now, he's going to give her one for "la Marcelle." She knows you shouldn't say "la Marcelle," knows it's not grammatically correct, but she'll never tell that to her uncle, it would annoy him. Marcelle is her grandmother. Since being widowed she wears black and doesn't smile and doesn't eat very much. "Come on then, Lolo," he says. He's in work overalls and rubber boots, with mud on his hands and holding a spade. She closes the latch to the rabbit shed and comes over. He tells her to choose a lettuce, she points to the best one, the one that hasn't been eaten by slugs. He's standing behind her. He digs in his spade ten centimeters from her foot and the handle is taller than she is, she remembers the stick that her grandfather whittled and then put a notch in every summer to see how much she'd grown. He touches her butt, she wants to turn around, does he want to make fun of her too, does he know that Claude calls her Fatta? But she can't, he's holding her firmly by the nape of her neck like Thérèse when she's skinning a rabbit, tugging on the skin with her other hand while the blood seeps over the fur. He pushes her nose against the wall of the lean-to, one hand still gripping her neck while the other unbuttons her shorts and slips inside her panties, "Say, you don't have any hair yet," he says, driving his fingers between her legs as he forces them apart, "it'll come," she's lost her balance, she'd fall if he weren't holding her, "you like that, don't you, you really like it, all girls like it," he pushes against her butt, groaning, she can feel the knife that Thérèse uses for jointing rabbits, feel it against her back, a tractor appears around the corner at the bottom of the road, the fingers tense between her thighs, hurting her, then they suddenly pull away, and do up one button. His muddy hand is covered with brown patches. He lifts her up onto the half-built wall.

"Wait for me there."

Her heart beats like a rabbit's when it's about to die, it feels as if it wants to burst through her warm skin.

She waits.

She mustn't disobey her uncle.

He'd be sad.
He'd be angry.
It's a high wall.

She waits.

He comes back and she hasn't moved. Her calves shiver in the sunlight. He's off to have a coffee with "la Thérèse," he'll take her with him, come on, then. He lifts her up and sets her on the ground as if driving in a spade. She walks along beside him. Her legs carry her. At the farm, with Thérèse, she doesn't risk anything.

Thérèse is standing in the living-room-cum-kitchen, heating the coffee on the big wood-burning stove. Her husband, Roger, has just parked the tractor in the shed and sits down heavily on the bench. His overalls are covered in dried manure slurry. His cheeks are a purplish red and he looks up at her without smiling. "Ah! Lolo, so here y'are with le Félix!" says Thérèse. "You here f'some hooch?" She laughs. She has a few teeth missing. Nicolas, the eldest son, is here too, with his wife who helps in the cowshed and doesn't like children coming to watch the cows being milked.

The child wants to go over to Thérèse by the fire, she doesn't see her so often now that she's had "the works"—she doesn't know what this illness is, but it's the reason the cows now stay in the lower field. She doesn't have time to walk around the table before her uncle pulls her by the arm, sits her down next to him on the bench, facing the others, and delves his hand deep into her panties again, between her thighs, making himself at home. The others freeze, all eyes on that buried hand, then on her, her face. She doesn't dare move. If the grown-ups aren't saying anything, then it's all okay. The lettuce sits before her on the table, it still has mud on it. Uncle Félix drinks his coffee calmly, pours a drop of the hard stuff into it with his left hand while his other hand rummages inside her shorts as if in his own pocket. The grown-ups pay no attention to him, they're staring at her. Dirty little thing, their eyes say. Even Thérèse's eyes have a different glint, there's a nastiness she's never seen before, just like the daughter-in-law with that twisted smile. They're passing judgment on her and it's bad, she can tell. But if it's bad, why don't they say something? She can't work out whom to smile to now. Balto comes over and sniffs her knee and tugs at her laces. Fainting—that would save her. But no. The afternoon drags on. She's a rag doll sitting on a bench, with a hand fumbling inside her panties for all to see. Shame smells of coffee. Fear stinks of dog. When it's over he stands in the doorway and sends her off with a pat on the butt, "Go on, scram, you go home now," sounding irritable as if she's been really annoying. Thérèse wipes the oilcloth without looking up. Roger puts his cap back over his gray hair and looks at his fly buttons as he rubs the back of his neck. On her way to her grandmother's house she deliberately walks through some stinging nettles, jumping into them and trampling on the lettuce, making it spout green blood.

She doesn't want to wear shorts anymore, she's stopped going to see the rabbits, she doesn't feel like eating vegetables now, she is scolded. She goes into her grandmother's bedroom one morning and tells her everything. Her grandmother stops sweeping, hunkers down on a level with her, and holds her by the shoulders as she says, "Don't ever tell anyone what you just told me. Do you understand? Never." The big yellow eiderdown on the bed is impeccably straight, not a single crease, she must have spent some time on it. The wooden furniture gleams, you can see your reflection in it. The word "never" is as heavy as the linen cupboard. Her grandmother goes back to her floor cloth, rubbing and scrubbing, she'll get the better of all this filth.

There's no card game that evening. Mommy's here, and Grandma, and Nana. There are two other people sitting around the kitchen table, there's Luce, an old cousin of Nana's who lives at the bottom of the village, and there's Auntie Berthe, one of her grandpa's sisters (so one of Félix's sisters too, she suddenly realizes), although—what's the opposite of a queen?—you'd hardly know she was a woman, she even has a mustache. It's called a family meeting, but it's more like a girls' meeting, she thinks, seeing as her father's in Rouen, he never comes down to La Chaux. Her grandmother must have summarized the situation already because no one asks her to go back over what happened. Anyone would think that it happened to the family, that it's something upsetting for the family, not to her, not for her. Her mother just asks if it hurt and did she bleed at all, making no attempt to check for sure. She doesn't look worried, she looks as if she's used to this. "He'd never go all the way," says Auntie Berthe, pinching her nose and eyeing her great-niece. She peers at the child as if trying to gauge what's under her rose-printed nightdress, her eyes have the same nasty glint as Thérèse's the other day. Claude left the kitchen as soon as she grasped that this was about Fatta, she's playing in the bedroom, humming to herself, you can hear the jacks rattling against each other, sometimes she hurls them onto the floorboards, "Not so noisy, Claude," Mom shouts, "we can't hear what anyone's saying!" "Of course he wouldn't go all the way," (*all the way where?*) says her grandmother. "It's just fiddling. Mind you: it's got to stop." "It's because of his wife," says the cousin, "it's ever since Jocelyne had the works." (The works? Like Thérèse? "What's the works, Nana?" she whispers to her great-grandmother who's knitting and hasn't yet said a word. "It's when they take the whole lot out," the old lady replies with a vague gesture toward her groin. She squeezes her nightdress between her thighs and feels like throwing up. "But not you, for goodness' sake, you dummy," Nana adds, patting her arm. "Old women.") "Since her operation, she just doesn't even want to talk about it and there's no room at the inn for her husband every night, so obviously he's frustrated. Men have their urges, it can't be helped. They need their bit of fun." "Fine, so what do we do about it?" "I'll have a quiet word with my brother," says Berthe, "I'll tell him to stop. As for you, Lolo, not a word, understand? Keep dirty laundry in the family. You forget about it, okay? Hush this up, our lips are sealed, all of us. If my sister-in-law found out about this it would be terrible for her, poor thing...She's done nothing to deserve this."

Her mommy takes her up to bed, tucks her in, and gives her a long kiss on her forehead. "You'll be fine, my darling. You go to sleep now." "What about the knife, Mommy, you didn't talk about the knife. If he knows I told on him, will he use it?" "It wasn't a knife, don't worry about it, you're not in any danger, my Lolo. The only thing you need to do now is avoid your uncle Félix. Whenever you see him, just go somewhere else, that's all. Then he'll leave you alone. And Auntie Jocelyne won't know a thing."

She says yes, okay, Mommy, closing her eyes to the kiss. "So, you been showing off?" Claude asks as soon as the light is out. "He already groped me, old Unky Félix, and I didn't make a whole thing of it. He's just a disgusting old man. You don't even have tits, anyway."

She struggles to get to sleep. What was it if it wasn't a knife? She pictures blood-soaked itty-bits operated on by surgeons, their hands covered in brown patches and holding needles and thread that they plunge into the flesh of the lips they're stitching up. She remembers what Auntie Berthe said, *Keep dirty laundry in the family.* Funny expression. All through the night washerwomen with mustaches beat the filth out of slurry-covered pants.

Over the next few days the women sit in the kitchen playing Scrabble and drinking verbena tea. She can hear their whispering through the wall. She's reading *Fantômette*, a story about a smart girl who solves every problem. Then one evening when she's already in bed with the light out, she's frightened when she recognizes Uncle Félix's laugh. "There's a last trick bonus!" he whoops. The following morning there's a bottle of Pernod on the table. Cards are more fun than Scrabble. But you need four people to play belote, that explains it, they can't do without him.

Her father doesn't know about this episode, and on their return to Rouen no one tells him the story, they don't even think to. In her grandmother's house she goes back to sit in her grandpa's armchair in front of the TV. Why's he the one who's dead, not Unky Félix, who's older than him anyway? Her grandmother says Maurice had his fourth heart attack when he insisted on carrying some lady's huge suitcase at the train station. After three cardiac episodes and at the age of sixty-three he followed his skirt-chasing heart, "and there you are, he left me all on my own. One glimpse of a petticoat and they're gone. Men really are the dumbest," she says in a bleating little voice.

5

Prince Charming vanishes from her dreams, so does the magic house. Her nights are populated by insects, they're infested with cockroaches and spiders that get into everything. Her body is full of holes through which it can be penetrated, her nightmares seethe. In her nana's copy of the newspaper *France Dimanche* she reads about a woman who had a headache for years and an X-ray eventually discovered an earwig eating away at her sinuses. It must have crawled up one of her nostrils when she was having a siesta in the countryside, the article explains. The child is haunted by these words. Every night she lies in the dark training herself to pinch her nose, close her lips, and press her thighs and buttocks tightly together: nothing must be able to get inside her, she's obsessed with the idea. One day she finds a little dead mouse in the water in the toilet; from then on, she won't go to the bathroom without a book that she flaps feverishly all around the bowl to shoo away anything that flies, moves, crawls, or penetrates. When she sits on the toilet she imagines herself seen from below, and her own eyes floating on the water see her as a gaping hole, she's so frightened she could scream, but *not a word*. She soon has to be treated for stubborn constipation, that's the word used on the note, "stubborn"—for once it's about her, not Claude. The remedy is worse than the complaint: suppositories and enemas...She thinks longingly of corks to block every entry, every exit—her body isn't a thoroughfare. There's no going in or out.

She doesn't like nightdresses, borrows Claude's pajamas and never takes off her panties; she's stopped washing, and only pretends to take a shower by turning on the water while she sits fully clothed on the edge of the tub. She eats with her teeth still clamped together, holding her hand over her mouth. She brushes her teeth carefully to avoid cavities, she doesn't want to go to the dentist and gape wide for Dr. Galiot. She doesn't like going for walks anymore, has stopped rolling around in the grass, and knows about all the dangers presented by insects. "Little critters don't eat big ones," Nana says. No, but they're sneakier: ticks bite into your skin and eat away at your nerves till you're paralyzed (she saw that once in La Chaux, it killed Balto's mother), as for wasps, if you accidentally swallow one when you're drinking, it stings you inside and kills you; even ants can colonize you and eat you up, hollowing you out till you're just an empty husk, a punctured balloon. Impenetrable—that's what she's going to be.

The next winter she has a large spot at the top of her thigh, under the elastic on her panties. She waits till it really hurts before telling her mother, and has to have an emergency procedure to remove the infected carbuncle with its seeping, inflamed head. Her father does it because he's a doctor. With his hands between her thighs he uses a scalpel to incise the engorged boil and release white pus. Her mother holds down both her arms to stop her moving. She wails. "You'll be okay, my little chicken, it's nothing much." Her father disagrees: a carbuncle's a dangerous thing, it could have killed her, why didn't she say anything? She cries. He covers her groin with a wad of gauze, which is instantly red with blood, and holds it in place with tape; it will need changing every day. "So, did you get your period?" asks Claude who has just started hers.

Nyah nyah nya-nya nyah…In the meantime, Claude may well have her period but she's regressing to childhood. One day she's brought home from school on a stretcher: she can't stand up. When the time came to get off her chair at the end of a French lesson, she couldn't do it, her legs wobbled, they couldn't hold her weight, and she collapsed. Aged thirteen, she's like a baby who needs carrying around. Her parents are worried. Having barely recovered from their younger daughter's carbuncle, they're confronted with the elder's paralysis—in fact, it's enough to make you think she too picked her moment to do a little party piece, but hey. It's difficult getting their parents' attention: they're always arguing these days, they say terrible things to each other, maybe they think the girls can't hear. Claude's illness has the advantage of reducing the yelling, for two weeks at least. The parents call a specialist who runs tests on Claude and declares, "There's nothing wrong with her." André tells Mom the same thing, "There's nothing wrong with her." And he adds, "It's just playacting to miss school." But Claude always collapses in tears as soon as anyone tries to stand her up. They go to see the leg specialist and he has a pair of hideous chunky shoes made, but Claude wears them only three times ("I should have gone into orthopedics," her father snaps when he receives the bill), they don't make any difference, she can't walk. One evening she cries and screams that she wants to die, she's so miserable that she rolls on the floor scratching her cheeks. She makes Daddy promise to stop telling Mommy she's good for nothing and lazy; she lies on the living-room sofa like a Merovingian king and makes him swear all sorts of things, he swears whatever she asks, that he'll take better care of her, that he loves her even if she doesn't believe him, he loves her more than anyone (great). So Claude gets up and goes back to school. He buys her a Circuit 24 electric car set for Christmas. Together on the living-room carpet they put together the metallic circuit that mimics the twenty-four-hour race at Le Mans, and every lunchtime, after the radio game show *Le Jeu des 1,000 francs*, they have Formula 1 races, feverishly working their joysticks. His car is blue, Claude's red. Occasionally one of the race cars derails because the corner's quite sharp; they laugh and then put it back on track right up until it's time for her to return to school and for him to do his home visits. Claude is proud and never stands aside: Fatta a race-car driver? Ha ha! Claude preens. Anyone would think their father belongs to her. But the truth is he soon reverts to yelling at their mother and going out in the evenings without a word, he doesn't keep his promises. It was just to get Claude back on her feet. Apparently in the nineteenth century there were women like Claude at the Salpêtrière hospital in Paris; young and old alike were paralyzed with no obvious cause, or mute, or even blind for no reason. They were labeled "hysterical"— an ugly word from the Greek for "uterus." What disease did they have? They didn't actually have anything. They had nothing, and that was their problem. Why did they have nothing where boys have something? They were devastated by this difference, they didn't fit the mold. It tormented them body and soul that they didn't know why. The whole story is explained in a book at the municipal library in Rouen, but it doesn't answer the question.

No one worries about *her* now, anyway—her carbuncle had hardly dried before Claude stole the limelight. Luckily, she still has Jeannine, but she doesn't tell her friend anything, she understands that she needs to keep it all to herself, especially the dirty laundry, particularly if you just can't seem to wash it. Now that they're at the big school, Jeannine likes commenting on what the boys are doing in their schoolyard. When they're not running around like rabid dogs, pretending to shoot each other or windmilling their arms in swordless sword fights, they come over to the fence between the two yards and call out to the girls. Jeannine stops her skipping or her hopscotch, so she does too, inevitably. The boys call them "sugar and spice" and Jeannine retorts with "snips and snails." She hangs back, even though she knows perfectly well they think she's prettier than Jeannine; at winter vacation camp there are always older boys wanting to carry her skis for her when she has trouble climbing to the drag lift. One time a big boy of at least thirteen offered her some Mon Chéri chocolates. "Well, I never..." one of the instructors said to another. "Yep," the other replied. "Shame she's only ten." "Don't you mean, it's just as well..." sniggered the first. She doesn't really understand what they're talking about and, still smiling sweetly (always smile, Nana says), she's on her guard, and when she remembers this later in the dormitory, she's sometimes stifled with fear. As for boys her own age, they don't do anything interesting. The only thing she envies them is their marbles, the red, blue, and yellow agates—she'd love to roll them around in her hand. But girls don't play marbles, that's just the way it is. Even her neighbor Joël whom she used to like is turning nasty; he catches a frog in his garden one day, sticks a straw up its ass and blows it up to make it explode. When it's half dead, he throws it into an anthill. He's not laughing but scowling, his face unrecognizable. She covers her eyes, she's cold, she feels like a frog. Frogs never turn into princes, all that's just stories, fairy tales.

She works very hard at school, she's always first or second in her class—she doesn't even like being second. Apart from Jeannine, every other girl becomes a rival, it's all about overtaking them. When she finishes an exercise before the others, which happens a lot, she pictures their itty-bits meekly shut tight in their panties, under their skirts and pinafores. She conjures an image of this row of slits lined up like desks and chairs, each one pierced by an inkwell— for dipping Sergent-Major pen nibs into. She's fascinated by the orderly repetition of this secret pattern hidden by the configuration of clothes and aped by the furniture, as if the ordinary visible world were a representation of an arcane forbidden world that she alone suspects. She's delighted that her thoughts are as invisible as these private parts. In the schoolyard she spots a tiny little blond girl who has just joined the elementary school. She herself is in fifth grade, with the big girls. She persuades Jeannine—who's a little reluctant because she'd rather spend recess poking fun at boys—to come with her to talk to this little girl, whose name is Louisette. At first she asks her for minor things, to bring her some candy or sing her a song, and Louisette sweetly complies. Then she tells her to wait for her in this part of the yard every recess, she forbids her from playing with the other girls in her class, and orders her to come to school with no panties on. She threatens Louisette with the worst forms of torture if she disobeys or talks to anyone about this. Sometimes Louisette cries, that's fine, it keeps you warm. Then one day it's not Louisette who's there to meet her by the restrooms under the covered yard but Madame Tournier, the teacher: Louisette has complained and if they don't stop upsetting her right now and once and for all, they will be expelled, Madame Tournier says. They mustn't talk to Louisette anymore, or even approach her. Understood? The teacher's expression is harsh, no one can have seen her face like this before; she—the girl who works so hard—certainly hasn't. "That doesn't entitle you to absolutely anything," says the teacher. "You should be ashamed." She has to obey but for a long time she's obsessed by the little blond girl with the cherubic face. She wishes she could chain her up. She wants to beat her for reporting her. She'll be leaving to move up to middle school at the end of the year so she calculates how long it will be before Louisette herself is in fifth grade, then she'll be able to start again, to punish her; but when that time comes, she herself will be leaving for high school in another part of town. This means that repeating a year would be the only way of regaining control, far from Madame Tournier's care. No way she'll give up Louisette. She'll repeat a year, she promises herself.

In the meantime, she develops a passion for reading the Comtesse de Ségur—when Sophie's mother says "You're a naughty girl" her face looks like Madame Tournier. She studies the illustrations in her books, analyzes the punishment scenes, the back-and-forth of dresses hitched up to reveal bare buttocks pitched high in air. She's never made to stand in the corner in class but the girls who are elicit a form of envy in her. Before going to sleep at night, she goes over and over the day when Annie scored zero in dictation and had to spend the whole day, even recess, wearing a dunce's cap. Everyone laughed and pointed at her, and she cried, burying her chin in her neck. From the start of this waking dream, she takes the role of the dunce, wandering about the street in that cardboard hat while others jeer. But her favorite dream is one she invented. It takes place in school. The principal of the boys' school is standing in for Madame Tournier who's sick so, just this once, the fifth grade is mixed. Today they have an object lesson. Object lessons usually revolve around something like dew, steam, or a walnut; last week, they studied eggs:

the yolk, the albumen, the membrane, and the pocket of air. The object for today is: a girl. Monsieur Brun writes it in chalk in big letters: A GIRL. Then he glances over the students and his eyes come to rest on her: "To the blackboard," he tells her. She stands up and walks past the rows of tables. "Take off your pinafore." She unbuttons it, keeping her eyes pinned on her shoes. "Lift up your dress and take down your panties." Some of the boys laugh, a few girls giggle. "Go on, faster than that! What a sluggard," says the teacher, yanking her panties down to her socks. Then he presses against her back and bends her, folding her in two over his desk, with her dress over her head and her panties around her ankles. He points to and names the various visible parts, then invites the students to file past to have a closer look at the ass and the asshole which he's pointing at with his cane. She's crying under her dress—"won't you be quiet, for goodness' sake"—so he lifts her feet one by one to pull off her panties and put them in her mouth. Now that she's gagged, he stands her back up, turns her around and continues with his object lesson. The boys file past again to see the other side: "She doesn't have any titties," says one, "Nah, but she's got a fat ass," says another. She shifts and moans: "You're disobedient," the teacher tells her. "And apparently you're top of the class?" He attaches her arms over the hook to the left of the blackboard, where the geography maps hang, and pulls her dress right up over her face, all she has now is her undershirt, eased up above her navel, her shoulders are rubbing against the map of France, she's choking. The bell rings, "Go on, all of you out!" yells the teacher. He takes his whistle, puts it in the pocket of his gray overalls, and leaves the room. She stays there, hanging by her arms with her panties in her mouth. It is usually at this point, as she lies in bed, that she feels a powerful wave thrilling through her thighs and stomach and then, a moment later, she passes out—well, she just isn't there anymore. It's only momentary but it's powerful, and the shame that goes with it feels good too. It was when she was scratching the scar left by her carbuncle, under the elastic on her panties, that she discovered this pleasure. With her thighs held tight at first, then opened, she laid hands on one hell of a find! And it never fails, all she has to do is conjure that image, the freeze-frame, her mouth gagged with her panties, the procession of prying eyes, there's always a moment when it wells up, it's coming, it explodes—more often than not the word "panties" is all it takes. She sometimes has a terrible headache, and wonders whether it will kill her, but she can see that it doesn't and starts over the following evening, or sometimes during the day, when she's alone.

She shares a bedroom with Claude and, once the lights are out, they often talk before going to sleep, so—now that her big sister is walking again—she tries to explain the object-lesson trick to her: she's discovered something incredible, a sort of Ali Baba's cave, an Aladdin's lamp that you just have to rub, it's fantastic, and she thinks Claude will stop treating her like a baby when she knows. Before revealing the whole Open sesame! to Claude, she makes her promise not to tell anyone about it, especially their parents. Claude promises. But she isn't convinced by the revelation. "I can't feel anything," she says. "Really? Try again. Rub it." "No, it's annoying. You're talking nonsense. And anyway, what's the connection with the object lesson? Do you think you're an egg or something?" They both giggle in the dark. "The idea is that *you*'re the thing, but *you* get to have the pleasure. Is it happening?" "No. Eggs don't have pleasure, Fatta. Come on, good night, Big Belly." She doesn't persist. So it's her own personal secret, then, a gift that only she has? A sort of return to the dream of the self-stocking house, but different: the candy and patent leather shoes are meaningless when you have this intense pleasure that can be repeated at will every day. So is she a unique sort of girl?

This seems to be view of the two women who turn up at their home just before dinner one evening. They're psychologists and are doing a study based on the results of tests run two months earlier within the Jeanne-d'Arc school community. They brazenly ask to see the apartment and go into "the girls' bedroom"—"Laurence doesn't have a room of her own, then?"—and the younger one makes notes in a spiral-bound book. "Are these Laurence's books on the shelf here? Does she read a lot? Has she had any illnesses? Any family incidents that need mentioning? And you, ma'am, you don't work, I imagine, do you look after your daughters? I'm now going to ask you to tell the girls to leave the room, we need to speak with you alone." "What's Fatta done?" Claude asks excitedly. "Has she done something bad?" But they're shoveled into the hallway, and the living-room door shuts out their curiosity. Luckily, they can hear everything through the wall. She's frightened. Are the ladies from the police? (She cheated on her geometry tests: she didn't understand any of it, but there were partially erased answers on the form so she copied them.) One of the ladies is talking about a queue: Isn't that like standing in line? Like a procession of schoolboys? Her heart beats harder, do psychologists know what's going on inside your head, can they guess your secret dreams? But no this is *IQ*, not *a* queue: the woman explains to her parents that IQ stands for intelligence quotient. Hers is high. Tremendous aptitude for language. Not so good at spatialization, but still, she has the highest score in the whole elementary-education community that was tested across Rouen. "Even compared to the boys?" her father's voice asks in amazement. "Yes. All students took the same tests." "Oh, I see. Well, I never..." "On the information sheet Laurence said that when she grows up she'd like to be a receptionist. Which was unexpected. Do you know why she put that?" "Oh, it must be because she saw them at the Paris Car Show, we went to the show, I'm fanatical about cars. She must have liked their uniforms, their makeup, I have to say they were very pretty." "That's normal for a little girl. But she can aspire to something better, you know. A better career." "Yes, of course. I'm always telling them they must get a job. But if I've understood your results correctly, she's not going to be the one to take over my office?" "Girls tend to be more literary, yes. Having said that, there are more and more women doctors, as you know." "Yes. But being a receptionist at an airport, for example, that would be good for Laurence. Languages are a good thing for girls to study, Russian, Chinese, there are plenty of prospects these days." "And your first daughter is how old, thirteen? Does she work as hard as her sister? Do they get along well?" "No, no, Claude's a lazybones, she does the absolute minimum, any excuse and she'll back off. Otherwise, well, you know what girls are like, they're always bickering, they pull each other's hair and so on. They can be real little bitches when they put their minds to it. Oh my, we could use some psychology…"

Claude slinks off to the bedroom to chew over the word "lazybones." For her, though, it's the word "bitch" that paralyzes her outside the living-room door then launches her into the bathroom where she shuts herself away. Why insult his own daughters, and in front of strangers? Because it *is* an insult, she knows that. But the ladies don't say anything. They thank her parents for their time and go on their way. "Goodbye, girls!" they call from the landing.

Their mother hasn't opened her mouth. Where on earth could this high IQ come from? From Matthieu, for sure, even if it doesn't show. He is a doctor, after all...As for her, she went to housekeeping school. Until now she wasn't allowed to exercise a profession without her husband's consent. The law has just changed and she'd like to earn some money, not have to ask for it from Matthieu every month, beg for it more like. She often helps him in his office when he's on duty, she's familiar with all of the patients' illnesses and treatments. But helping your husband doesn't count, that's not real work, especially with no qualifications. The point is this IQ of Lolo's is strange. Maybe it comes from her own father? You can almost hear the word "ingenious" in engineer.

Bitch. The word comes back and haunts her. It's an insult. But surely first and foremost it's a female dog? Anything female is a disappointment, a deficiency, she knows that now. Dog is a statement. Bitch is a judgment. Just change the gender and the word becomes nasty. But it has certain powers. She soon comes across it at the municipal library where she spends many hours at every opportunity. "Heliogabalus sometimes harnessed two stags to his coach, and on one occasion four dogs, and even once four naked bitches, making them tow him around," she happens to read in a book by Montaigne. These words go into the private anthology of her most violent intimate caresses. She has a sort of hit parade, like for songs. And this is a good sentence, stronger than the Comtesse de Ségur, she can see the image with that spat-out word, she can picture the girl on a leash walking on all fours, she can picture the animal being whipped and moving forward, she can picture herself in it. Being a bitch is something to enjoy, a pleasure. "Pleasure *vb.*: Give sexual enjoyment or satisfaction to." She first saw the word used in this way in a novel with a girl's name as a title—*Justine* or *Juliette*. She borrows all sorts of books from the library and a hybrid world takes shape; its main trajectory is that doctors in white coats marry nurses, that orphans find their fortune and happiness after a lot of misfortune and unhappiness, that girls by the name of Alice or Fantômette solve enigmas, and princesses are loved to distraction. It's different in her secret sentences, gathered at random across the shelves, it's the exact opposite even, like day and night; and yet the two worlds coexist, parallel but equally real. She believes in both. She is a thing, an animal, a queen of hearts, a princess, an idol, and a slave. She is humiliated and adulated, contemptible and top of the class. Her whole life is related in books. She is eleven years old.

6

She is eleven, Claude fourteen. Claude now receives mail, which is intercepted by their father, letters from boys who talk about her breasts and arrange to meet her in the changing rooms at the ice rink; so it's high time a responsible father explained the facts of life to his daughters. First, they need to know what sexual intercourse is. He draws a picture on a sheet of paper, it looks like a diagram of a kitchen sink. For sexual intercourse you need a boy and a girl. It's also called coitus—from the Latin *coire*, "to go with." (No, this particular Latin isn't in *Asterix*.) The basic premise they need to remember above anything else is that, actually, you *mustn't* go with a boy. Girls don't go with boys, period. That's it. (Really? Well, why's it called that then?) Not now, anyway. (When?) When they're grown up, when they have husbands, it'll be different then. They'll be allowed to. It will even be their duty to. He watches their mother clearing the table, it's not clear whether she's listening, but she already knows all this anyway. For now they must avoid boys who want to go with them, it's the only thing boys are after, but they—the girls—must resist, and the best way to do that is to ignore boys, not to reply when they talk to you or send you letters, not even to look at them. They should never under any circumstances end up alone with a boy, is that understood? "If you heat up a chestnut, it'll explode," he concludes. The image is a little obscure and essentially means: stay on your guard, coitus can happen so quickly. "But why do boys want this coy tuss?" "Because it feels good to them," her father says reluctantly. "But it doesn't for girls?" Claude asks, surprised, with a sideways glance at goody-goody Fatta who's pretending she has no idea what they're talking about—how about discussing that object lesson? "Girls are different," says their father (yes, we noticed). "In the early days it's not very nice for them. Coitus in fact consists of the boy's penis, also known as the phallus" (dick, pecker, prick, translates Claude who's already received quite a few letters from boys; member, shaft, dagger, translates Lolo who's already read quite a lot of Sade) "penetrates the girl's hole, which is called the vagina" (pussy, clam, temple of Venus, Mother Nature's altar). "Now, girls have a membrane at the entrance to the vagina; it's called a hymen, a word that also means 'marriage'" (this is getting ridiculous), "and when the penis is introduced it tears the hymen, which bleeds. But only once," their father reassures them. "That's virginity. Girls are virgins. All of them, to start off with. Oh, and the best example is Jeanne d'Arc—don't let's forget we live in Rouen. The Maid of Orleans. In this instance, maid means virgin, it means she's pure." "Is that the opposite of whore?" "Be quiet when I'm talking. And don't use dirty words. The first time is called deflowering. It happens on the wedding night." "Does it hurt?" "No, not much," says their father (*their father knows everything*). "It doesn't last long." "And what's this disfloweration for? Why would anyone want to get rid of flowers?" she asks. Her father throws his head back and laughs, but that's kind of what's going on: the husband mows down all the flowers on the first night, then he can be sure he's the first, and he wants to be the first. She pulls a face. So she'll be like the lawn razed bare of daisies when her father's trundled up and down it with the lawn mower? "What about him, the husband? How do you know you're the first for him?" "It doesn't matter with him. Quite the opposite." The equivalent of virginity in a girl is experience in a boy. These values are inversely proportional in a couple: she must be ignorant, he knowledgeable, that's the principle. With girls, the less they know, the more they're respected (except for Justine, but hey, her father doesn't know every girl there is). On the wedding night the husband needs to know what to do, that's what's expected; the wife, on the other hand, just has to take it lying down. So marriage is pretty similar to the object lesson, when all's said and done. Any questions? No no.

The answers are in *The Guide to Sex* which Claude soon orders under a fake name, and in which there are several words their father doesn't know. These will be the object of close examination: orgasm, clitoris, and masturbation. (Aha! You see, it does exist!)

It soon becomes clear that virginity really is their father's pet subject. And this isn't so much to do with the business about purity—he's a Protestant and Protestants don't give a fig about the Virgin, at least that's what she gleaned from her first years of Bible study. No, what he's obsessed with is them falling pregnant (because you fall, you fall so low you can never get back up). Them having a bun in the oven, a plane in the hangar, bacon in the drawer, a pea in the pod, them being late, up the pole, knocked up, in the pudding club, with child, in the family way, in a delicate condition, wearing the bustle the wrong way, harboring a fugitive, eating for two. Girls are the millstones around their fathers' necks. He doesn't really know how to go about this, to coerce them or to convince them, but his prevaricating is wasted: it's neither. He's especially worried about Claude: she already has her period and wears bras, and she screams if he comes into the bathroom without warning. Lolo, well, she's still a little girl. Oh yes, he forgot to explain that periods are proof that you're not pregnant. Girls are in fact governed by the moon. Their cycle follows the moon's, twenty-eight, maybe thirty days, that's why their moods are so changeable, they're what you'd call "lunatics," they're not truly free, they depend heavily on nature. Claude sniggers but Laurence scowls: her father often uses the expression "moon-faced idiot." So it's not some great gift to be associated with the moon. "Are boys the sun, then?" (*Is it the sun that makes these brilliant boys so brilliant?*) "No, boys aren't governed by nature, they master it, they tame it. When *they* bleed, it's in war, it's when they fight." (*Well, fine, but they also have nosebleeds, and you have to listen to them howling at school when they get the smallest owie on their knee.*) "Girls have to accept the concept of a cycle, of periods and being regular. It's natural, period! What this means first and foremost is not being late." Late = pregnancy = exploded chestnut = whore. She looks nervously at the clock on the kitchen wall, unaware that these words will soon become a catchphrase for her and her sister: I'm late, I'm running late, how late are you? "So at the end of the day," their father continues, "it's not complicated. Let's recap: you just have to be good and obey your father. Girls have their periods, it's a rule of nature, and they follow the rules. End of story."

That night the story is elaborated. A new object lesson: chestnuts. The scene is blood-soaked, knives spring up, threatening to pop the cork, to burst the chestnut. She lets herself be bled like a piglet, tied to the ladder in La Chaux where every summer she sees a pig empty its blood into a bowl, blood that is then used to make black pudding. She's on her stomach with a thick chafing rope binding her ankles and wrists to the rungs of the ladder, she's powerless to escape the implements and fingers and insects penetrating her, or the laughter humiliating her. She's in pain and people are laughing at her: "Are you making black pudding, then?" During the day her mind is full of questions but it finds no answers. When a boy and a girl are allowed to (when they're married), they "go together," they have coy tuss. Fine. And what about love in all this? People say "making love," but why? What's the connection with their father's explanations? Where does "I love you" fit into the operating instructions for the pipe-work? Screwing, fucking, getting laid, banging, okay. But at what stage do you tell each other yes, yes, I want to marry you, yes, I love you, yes, I want to, yes? How do lovers get to the coy tuss? She now knows what making love means, but she doesn't know what love is, or how you know it's love, if it is.

There are novels of course. The Marquis de Sade isn't very informative on the subject. In *The Famous Five*, Anne is a little in love with her cousin Francis but that doesn't help Laurence's understanding much either. She takes out Guy des Cars's *Les Filles de joie* from the library. She chose it because its mysterious title associates girls with joy, and you don't see that every day, but as she keeps reading, she realizes that the story is in fact sad. There's no joy for girls anywhere in books, except in the children's section where she's almost completely stopped looking, and the Harlequin collection that she skims through avidly without finding any elucidation: she isn't poor and there isn't a single millionaire around, so the prerequisites for love don't appear to have been met.

She moves into sixth grade. The school has only recently become mixed—in her mother's day it was a school for girls, the sign over the front gate still says so. Boys are in a minority but that isn't obvious. They show off in the schoolyard, they shout and pull girls' braids, and even though they're not as good at their schoolwork, she notices that they're quick to raise their hands and give stupid replies. They're kind of ridiculous with their Bermuda shorts, their puny little calves, and their jeering, but they don't know this. Their voices change and swoop up to a higher register in spite of their best efforts—truth be told, they don't seem that great at taming nature.

On Sundays she goes to the skating rink. She doesn't have breasts, she wishes she had her Barbie doll's breasts but it's not looking promising. She stuffs cotton wool into a bra borrowed from Claude. In the absence of breasts, she does have Barbie's hair, long blond hair that helps hide the lack of breasts, and she refuses to have it cut, even by one centimeter. When boys invite her to skate around the rink with them, they mostly talk about her sister. As a whole, they're not rocket scientists, but some of them have scooters to get out of Rouen. When she refuses to take their hands as they get onto the ice, some of them skate off toward another girl, shouting, "You're ugly, anyway" (she couldn't care less, she knows it's not true), or even, if they know her name, "Flat-chested lard ball" (and that hits home but she gives them a dismissive smile). She's particularly interested in the boys who are interested in her sister, either to pour scorn on them in front of her, or to pour scorn on her in front of them. Claude no longer calls her Fatta but Goody-goody. But Claude is actually the hypocritical one who celebrated her confirmation at the temple with all the bells and whistles just so she could be given a scooter, but on her retreat she'd practically roasted Louis's chestnut, Louis was the handsomest of the catechumens—it's all in her private diary that she hides under her mattress with *The Guide to Sex*. The whole Protestant family comes up from the Ardèche for her first Communion, with their prayers and gifts for Claude who plays the virgin in her white dress. During the celebratory meal in a big Rouen restaurant, their father says "my girls" several times in conversation with their aunts and uncles who hardly know them. It occurs to her that he seems happy. And is drinking a lot of champagne. "So there are two nuns sheltering from the rain under a porch on the place de la Madeleine. Leaning against the wall next to them is a prostitute wearing tons of makeup, a miniskirt, and fishnet hose. The nuns look at her, hesitate, and then one of them ventures 'Excuse me, ma'am, I'd like to know—how much do you charge, um, for your work?' The prostitute replies: 'For a trick? No special requests? Well, that's two hundred francs.' The nun turns to the other nun and says, 'I told you the curate swindled us with that bar of chocolate, sister.'" The joke may well bash papists, but it doesn't make the Huguenots laugh. "Stop it, Matthieu, not in front of the girls." "What's the difference between a woman and a swimming pool? Anyone? Do you give up, Uncle Léon? Well, there's no difference at all, they're both far too expensive considering how much time you get to spend in them!" "Matthieu, the girls!" The Calvinists are choking. She herself isn't sure what her father can be thinking, treating them like the inhabitants of a convent one minute and buddies from military service the next. It must be because he hasn't entirely given up hope of having boys, while still acknowledging that he has girls... "Come on, they need to learn about life," he retorts, pouring himself another glass.

Life.

This is life.

Jokes. Laughter.

What about love?

She still doesn't know. The mystery is growing. One day, she asks Nana what it's like, being in love, how you know, but Nana's not the right person: she had Grandma without having a husband, when she was very young, a teenage mom, they call it, or a single mother—it's like a chestnut that burned as it exploded, and no one wants to eat it now. Before she started her perfumery, Nana was a seamstress, and there are only two things she can explain to her great-granddaughter: First of all, always wanting to look presentable—not pretentious or flashy, showing off with trinkets and flounces, no, just presentable, in "a well-ironed dress, and clean socks and panties, in case you're in an accident, that makes you presentable." In short, presentable means you can be presented to anyone, even death, without feeling embarrassed. And second, with the help of the first element, the need to marry before turning twenty-five. "If not, if you're still single when you hit that milestone, you've had it, you'll be on the shelf." On the shelf? "Yes. An old maid. A spinster if you prefer. When I was a seamstress, we'd make yellow and green hats every Saint Catherine's day, and we'd pray to her, to that virgin and martyr who was the patron saint of old maids, asking her to send us a husband soon. But you're so pretty," Nana adds, "you won't have that problem."

Presentable, fine. A husband, okay. Before turning twenty-five, noted. But love? Someone who loves me?

Her mother's the one she needs to ask. She spends time by the window, and studies herself in the mirror in new dresses, she learns Italian, "the language of love," she calls it, and runs every time the phone rings. And sometimes cries. *She* must know.

She once knew, in any event. She has known. Maybe it's a little too late to ask her. She'd had enough of begging for money from Matthieu every month and has found work in an import-export office, and goes away for holidays in Capri with André, but he's just had a third child with his wife, a little boy called Jules, so, as the song goes, "Capri, c'est fini." She buys books that are discussed on the radio, Évelyne Sullerot's *La Femme dans le monde moderne* (Women in the Modern World), and novels by Benoîte Groult and Françoise Sagan. She also gets hold of *Lettre ouverte à une femme d'aujourd'hui* (Open Letter to a Contemporary Woman) by André Soubiran because the author's name is André and because she wants to stop taking valium. "The mental integrity of twentieth-century women is under threat. They are no longer the women of yesteryear whose world was confined to children, cooking, and church, but they don't yet know what the woman of tomorrow will be," says the copy on the cover. She just keeps taking pills ending in "-um" to help her sleep, ones ending in "-am" to relax her, and ones ending in "-ine" to dull her pain—she asks her husband for the prescriptions. When he forgets she screams appallingly and leans over the balcony rail, nobody loves her, she's had enough of this life. "Mommy, Mommy," the girls cry, "what's wrong? Come on, come back in, Mommy, close the window!" "What's the matter?" asks their father. "Is Aunt Flo visiting?"

In seventh grade Laurence discovers the great playwrights Racine and Corneille, who confirm the intuition gleaned from her mother: love is when you want to die. It's not cheerful, but in plays there's always something to stop you doing it: it's the verse, it's the rhyme, the pleasure of recurrence, of what goes around coming around, of what always eventually returns—sounds and words and hope. "I loved, my lord, I loved: I wanted to be loved." She discovers Louise Labé's sonnets, "I live and die; I am burned and I drown." She speaks out loud ten times, twenty times, declaiming words of love, lodging them in her brain. She learns the meter, the codes, the characters. There's a beauty in the rules, the regularity and repetition, a poetry; and there's something miraculous about girls imitating the moon. She cries over songs and poems, and writes a few of her own. When she goes to Jeannine's house, she reads the music magazine *Salut les copains*—Jeannine has a subscription and cuts out photos of Claude François and Joe Dassin, to stick them into a notebook next to the song lyrics. One time she brought home a seven-inch single by Johnny Hallyday that Jeannine gave her, but then she forgot it on the turntable in the living room. When her father found it he almost broke it in two, saying the lyrics were obscene. "Obscene *adj.*: Offensive or disgusting portrayal of sexual matters." She's surprised and wonders if Johnny is inadvertently more obscene than Sade. What they mostly listen to on Jeannine's Teppaz record player is Sylvie Vartan, "*I wear my hair long, like a boy, and a leather jacket, like a boy, a gold medallion and a big chunky belt, like a boy.*" There's a photo of her in the magazine, she's astride a big motorbike, her hands defiantly on her hips, but at the end of the day, "*I'm just a girl,*" goes the chorus, "*do what you want with me, and that's the best it can be, you see-ee-ee-ee.*" What would be amazing would be to win the prize in the teen magazine *Mademoiselle Âge tendre*: the first prize is an invitation to the millhouse where Claude François—otherwise known as Cloclo—lives. His actual house! He sings, "*You're so sweet, my Candy, Candy, you know your mouth's like sugar, and you make your kisses sweet, oh, yes your skin is really so, your mouth is just so sweet,*" and they join in the chorus as they gobble Tagada strawberry candy, which makes your mouth red and appropriately sweet—but actually, no, in the last few weeks Jeannine has stopped eating candy, it makes you fat, and if she wants to be the next Miss *Âge tendre*, she'd better lose some here and here, and here too, all over the place in fact, "I need to lose it," she keeps saying, "I absolutely have to lose." On her way home from Jeannine's house, taking the packet of Tagada strawberries with her, Sylvie's chanted words pound in

Laurence's head like a metronome, *I'm just a girl, see-ee-ee-ee*. She's still singing it to herself in bed in the evening. Something's bothering her, but what is it?

On the subject of metronomes, Laurence is behind schedule in the plumbing department. She's not yet "formed," as the doctor puts it. Is something changing shape? She tells lies at school, gathering snippets of expressions from her mother and Claude and wearily telling her friends or the sports teacher "I'm indisposed" or "I have a stomachache." Sometimes the teacher gets angry. "So what?" he asks Claude who brought the permission slip. "That never stopped anyone from doing the high jump." "What does he know about it, the asshole?" snaps her mother who, since she started working, curses a lot more and says funnier things. The teacher even calls Jeannine "an actress" when she's contorted with pain every month, and he puts "unjustified absences" on her school report. Jeannine has read that your periods stop if you don't eat, so she puts two fingers down her throat in the restroom after meals and throws everything up, but it doesn't change anything, except that it's good for her figure. Laurence does the opposite, eating to make her periods finally come. She doesn't envy her friend's cramps but she's had enough of Claude calling her a baby. When she was little, she saw her mother rinsing out clots of blood over the bidet and stuffing big cumbersome pads between her legs or, later, like Claude she used oblong wads of cotton wool wrapped in netting. The blood runs red, just like a knee when you fall off your bike, but is slightly thicker and it browns in the open air. Depending on the timing, it smells like a butcher's shop or an insipid flower—sickeningly so. It lasts five days and comes back every month. Imagine falling off your bike every month! The number of dressings! Her mother gets them from the drugstore each month, they're pretty expensive. In the long run it'll cost Daddy an arm and a leg having a wife and two daughters. Sometimes you'd think he was keeping an eye on the packets, especially Claude's, she's already seen him counting, he's checking the output. Mom also buys smaller boxes—of tampons—but girls aren't allowed to use them, they could break their hymens and they wouldn't even know. Imagine the shame on their wedding night! Laurence thinks that if Unky had exploded the chestnut, her father would have been told, he would have thought it was obscene and things would have heated up. But, phew, she still has it, she still has her cork, even though your period can get past it—she doesn't really understand how, it can't be exactly watertight, but nature's clever like that, apparently.

Periods are like wiener and foofoo, there are tons of words to say the same thing, it's laughable. When their parents are arguing, for example, her father always ends up asking whether she's on the rag. He also says, "Pissing out blood." "It was pissing out blood," he might say about someone brought to his office in an emergency. So the blood comes from the same place as pee, she registers, but not from the moment you're born: you have to wait till you're older. "You'll be a big girl soon," her grandmother tells her. She finds blood disgusting but also can't wait to be like the others, to be the same as Claude and her mother, to be conjugated in the feminine. I'm expecting my monthlies, you've got your lady time, she's surfing the crimson tide, we're on the rag, you (plural) have a visit from Aunt Flo, they're on the blob, it's their time of the month, they have a code red, their monthly visitor, their lady friend, lady days, lady business, Bloody Mary, shark week, the red army has landed, the redcoats have landed. We girls pay our respects to the moon, cross the Red Sea, are a bit off-color, are out of sorts, not ourselves, have a bad week, have the curse.

"Okay, fine," says Jeannine's cousin who wants to marry her when she grows up. "Okay, it's a curse. But it's only five days a month. But *we* have to shave every day. And we have military service too."

One morning, a dark-haired man brushes past her and just as he reaches her, he grabs her butt, digs in his fingernails, and whispers something in her ear before continuing on his way. She has to stop, right there on the sidewalk, suffocating. "He's a *bicot*," says the woman at the newspaper stand who saw everything, "those *crouilles* are all sex maniacs." She doesn't know either of these words and can't find them in the *Quillet* encyclopedia so she asks her father about them. "Don't use those words," he tells her, "they're slang, it's vulgar. The man must have been one of those hundreds of Algerians that the bosses at the Renault factory have been bringing over in the last few years to work at Cléon," he explains. "They left their whole families behind so they don't have their women and they miss them, that's why they have wandering hands. Even the whores don't want anything to do with them," he adds, laughing. "Take Skinny Minny, for example, when she comes to my office for the clap, she's very clear on that, 'I have my pride,' she says." "So what should I do then?" "Cross to the other sidewalk," her father replies. "In broad daylight you shouldn't be in too much danger. What were you wearing? And don't go out in the evenings. But to be really safe: the minute you see a sleazy-looking man, cross the street." And because she's looking thoughtful (isn't the word "whore" slang? and "the clap"?), he calls her and Claude into the living room at the end of the meal and shows them some self-defense techniques. Then he acts out a scene. "Okay, I'll be the attacker," he says, grabbing Claude by the arm. "Go ahead, escape me. Well, pretend to, I mean," he clarifies with a grimace. Claude loves this game. "A hard kick in the balls, and no hesitating," she says, not for the first time. "The guy's on the ground for a while," she adds gleefully. "D'you get it, Laurence? You aim for the rocks. Could you do that?" her father asks. "Straight at the family jewels." She says yes, yes, as she pictures diamonds and pearls—she definitely doesn't want to try, not with her father. It's reassuring to know a boy's weak spot, to know where you can really hurt them, by all accounts. But at night in her dreams she can't do it, she doesn't even think about it. In her dreams, the attacker wins, every night. And he has his revenge.

She has her first period at last, almost a year later than everyone else. She's glad. "That's that for the next forty years, my darling," her mother says with a smile that doesn't reach her eyes. "So, did it happen?" Claude taunts, "You're no longer a baby? Welcome to the club, Fatta." Her mother protests: she doesn't want Claude to call her sister Fatta now that Jeannine's in the hospital. Without breathing a word to anyone, she completely stopped eating, she weighs thirty-three kilograms, doesn't go to school anymore, and might die. No one's allowed to visit her, not even her mother, apparently, it's sad. In natural sciences, they're studying the reproductive cycle of frogs—a word of warning here: toads are not the male to female frogs, absolutely not, that's a common misconception. There are male and female toads, and male and female frogs. It's the females (the girls) who deal with reproduction, always and everywhere. Those two extra letters—the "fe" of female—sure do have a lot of work to do. And reproduction is a strange expression. In a way, it's the opposite of death, but it doesn't work like a photocopier: it's not an identical reproduction. For example, girls aren't machines, they don't just inanely reproduce themselves. Sometimes they make boys.

She's bored at middle school, French is the only subject that wakes her up. She dreams of being a Corneille or Racine heroine, recites Lamartine to herself and coils herself around words of love. All the teachers are women, except for sports and manual work. The men never use students' first names, only their family names, sometimes prefixing them with a sarcastic "Miss." In the seventh grade, Mr. Renard teaches the girls to sew; they make aprons and velvet-covered coat hangers edged with braid; they knit and baste and hem. He sometimes asks one of the students to stitch a button back on his shirt or to iron his tie. "Miss Barraqué, you seem to be struggling with your pattern, so come see me." At the back of the room, the boys are studying electrical circuits or diagrams of engines. When the boys play soccer during phys ed, the girls work on the gymnastic beam, and on these occasions the male teacher hands them over to his female colleague, a spinster who must weigh more than a hundred kilograms and isn't much more sympathetic on the subject of monthlies—she must have forgotten what they're like, apparently when you're old you stop having them. In shot put the girls have to manage three meters, the boys five, that's the way it is and that's final. Laurence has really strong arms but is very careful not to go over three meters and tries to avoid inevitable puns and giggles about her family name, which sounds so like beefy or hunky. At night, Mr. Renard comes to give object lessons—"Barraqué, to the blackboard!"—then he whips her naked ass until it bleeds in front of the whole class because the fly button that he asked her to sew back on has come off again.

7

One day at the swimming pool, she's lying on the grass reading, alone. Claude has already left with her gang, and Laurence is pretending to be an only child. Jeannine died in the spring, she weighed 28 kilograms, there was so much she wanted to lose that she ended up losing her life. At thirteen, Laurence now isn't really sure why she's here. Boredom becomes blurred with fear. At seven o'clock the bell rings to announce closing time. She looks up from her book. A few meters from her a boy is putting his clothes back on—she's never seen him before. He's already put on his pants and, holding his polo shirt in one hand, he's watching the sun start to go down. He has his back to her, his waist is accentuated by a leather belt, then lines of muscle widen toward his shoulders. The words in the book she's reading suddenly make her throat dry, the sentence describing the knight Tristan, whom the queen loves: "his shoulders wide and his flanks lean." And all at once it's him, he's Tristan from the story, freshly delivered to the Saint-Saëns pool. Gazing at him like the drop cap in the title on the book cover, she can't breathe properly, she's hot and cold at the same time, there's a stone weighing down on her chest, and her heart's beating fast, but down in her belly. The boy turns around, he has hair on his chest, he's at least sixteen years old, maybe seventeen; he catches her watching, their eyes meet, he gives her a little wave, she looks away, not acknowledging the gesture. But still. He picks up his sports bag and walks away, she watches him leave. His back. His shoulders. Oh, to run, to stop him, press yourself to him, put your hands on his arms, around his neck, and for him to accept her, to welcome her, to want her. For him to beg her. She stays there on her towel, motionless, her throat dry, thunderstruck. Under her skin there's a feeling like nothing she's known.

Afterward she forgets.

Then it comes again—it's intoxicating, the same feeling, intact and vital, and new, an incoming tide that both freezes her and brings her to life, that irrigates and desiccates. For her birthday her grandmother buys her a ticket to a Maurice Béjart ballet: "Such a nice present for a girl." At first she focuses on the dancing itself, no relation to the little trainees at the Opéra who still fuel her ambitions. All at once the whole stage is occupied by one bare-chested male dancer wearing heavy eye makeup, she watches him, his chest is transplanted into hers, there in the second row, he's all she can see. It's Jorge Donn, in twenty-five years he will die of AIDS but for now he's twenty. She likes the fact that he's muscly and wearing makeup, athletic and feminine, effeminate, her father would say, that he has long eyelashes and a protective shield between his thighs, she likes a boy not being the opposite of a girl but including her, comprising her. Boys are her opportunity, she senses it. And yet they're still a poignant enigma; their beauty is an arrow in her heart, and her stomach is now permanently tattooed with a male imprint.

From this point on everything's different. The nocturnal object lesson doesn't disappear, but her days are filled with a new knowledge: she's not just a thing, she's a girl. Boys are now the lesson, and she's very keen to learn it: their shoulders, their chests. The word "chest," the word "shoulders," the words "muscles," "boy," and "man"—they all arouse in her a particular sensation that doesn't yet have a name; it isn't the solar explosion of her nights spent hanging on other words, harnessed to other images, but it's a promise. A promise of what or whom she doesn't know. Is it the fairy-tale prince she still reads about? Perhaps. But right now he's naked, and the bittersweet pain that his presence and his absence provoke gnaws at her ribs. His chest wrenches her heart, his back, a sign with its converging lines, illustrates the thing she's missing. And so she discovers desire, several years after discovering pleasure. This absence makes her feel alive, while the night leaves her dead. Climaxing eliminates her, yearning brings her to life. Pleasure is fleeting but desire goes on forever. Life deprived of everything, death fulfilled by nothing. Given that she's experienced the nothing, she now needs to master the everything. What's it like, exactly? This was not discussed in her father's object lesson. The sun shimmers, the grass grows greener. She never expected it, but one day her prince will come—she hasn't forgotten the song.

Do you remember her, that girl and the shattering way desire burst into her life? Yes, I remember her. The new world order suddenly takes shape and acquires meaning: boys are made for her. They're different, of course, but that's just it, that's the challenge, the adventure. They're young and handsome. Their muscles ripple under their skin and they have an anxiety in their eyes and smiles, even when they're insolent. What on earth could be more urgent than cleaving her girl body to them? I remember that troubled intoxication, that informed ignorance. "Oh, how shall we suffer, my Lord, when so many seas lie between us?" Everything is suddenly clear. You just have to reduce the distance to zero. To move, at last, from being presentable to being presented. To make yourself present. But how? Luckily, my sister has a more reliable understanding of all this, she's sixteen. She also has a boyfriend, although she doesn't want to go out with him (she has her eye on someone else), so she's happy to hand him on to me, for a trial run, "to see if it works," she says. Out of nowhere I've become interesting in her eyes, I can tell—don't let's forget the secondary benefit of being reunited with my sister. "His name's Romain, he'll never set the world on fire but he's a good kisser," Claude tells me. Okay, but I've never canoodled with anyone—"canoodle" is one of Mom's words—so I don't know how to kiss. No need to worry about that, Claude will teach me. She sits me down next to her on the living-room sofa, puts her arms around my shoulders and sticks her tongue in my mouth; I recoil a full meter away from her. "Well, yes, are you dumb or something? You use your tongue otherwise it's just a peck, I'm talking about French kissing here, smooching, snogging, smackers!" I come back over and she does it again, she churns her tongue inside my mouth and I don't know what to do with mine. "You just turn yours too, well, you let it turn itself, it happens naturally." I put my mind to it and yes, yes, I'm starting to get this. I like it. "Okay, you're there, Fatta, I'm calling Romain," my sister announces.

Romain isn't very good-looking, but he has a motorbike. He's not exactly clever either but who cares. I'm thirteen, he's eighteen; he takes me at breakneck speed into the Normandy woodland, and we kiss furiously on the mouth behind the fences. I ask him if he's slept with a girl yet and he says yes. I like it when it's hot and he takes off his shirt to lie tanning himself on the green grass. His back is smooth and white, a little too smooth and a little too white to be manly, but still...When he tries to unbutton the top of my blouse, I say no and put my hands over my breasts, well, over the breast area, then I say no again, hoping he'll understand that that's a yes but I still need to have the object lesson—is there pleasure to be gained from agreeing? As soon as he hears the word "no" he stops and straightens my blouse to reassure me. He says he respects me, and I'm too young. I think he's happy to be the first person to kiss me, and that's enough for him, he's not gunning for "disfloweration." I don't tell him that the first boy I kissed was actually my sister. That kiss brought us closer together, Claude and me. We're starting to confide in each other. One Sunday morning, I'm sitting on her knee and we're both in our nightdresses whispering things to each other, when Nana comes in without knocking. Her whole face changes at the sight of us. "Not two girls!" she wails. "Not two girls together, that's sinful!"— and she hauls me by the arm to get me away from my sister. Claude howls with laughter and follows her down the corridor. "But would a girl and a boy be fine, Nana? Go on, tell us, is it okay if it's a boy?"

The problem is old men. The ones who are over thirty. There's one when we're coming out of school, he wears a dirty raincoat that he opens when we walk past, revealing a tiny little thingamabob that he tugs at as if hoping to lengthen it. Every now and then the headmistress shoos him away, flapping her hands at him, but he always comes back. A gaggle of four or five girls sometimes plow toward him arm in arm out of curiosity. I cross the street, a fossil-ized fear resurfaces, even if I do now know the difference between a winkle and a knife.

Since learning how to kiss, I've made sure I don't lose the knack. I trawl garage parties with Sylvie, a girl in my class. She has a sister called Viviane who's two years older than us and who, unlike my sister, lets her go with her to surprise parties where there are older boys, some even have their driver's license and play guitar. We shake our hair around when we dance, and wear corduroy pants, Clarks shoes, and Peruvian tunics, and wait till the ladies' choice to kiss the handsomest boy. One summer Sylvie and her sister go camping in their grandmother's garden in Coutainville with some friends of Viviane's who've just finished their end-of-school exams. I just got top grades in my *brevet* at the end of middle school. Reassured by the grandmother's presence, my father agrees that I can join them, on the con-dition that I sleep in the house, of course, and not pell-mell in a tent, "Is that understood?"—if you heat a chestnut, it'll explode. He briefs the grandmother over the phone and she says "Yes, of course" to all his recommendations; she's deaf and the batteries in her hearing aid have run out, she wouldn't hear a chestnut explode at arm's length.

When I get to the beach, with my backpack still on from the bus journey, I see Viviane with her boyfriend Gérard rubbing sun cream on her, and three other boys chatting. Sylvie and her cousin Catherine are in the sea. Viviane introduces me with a wave of her hand: "Laurence, a friend of my sister's." The boys—Franck, Hervé, and Daniel, "hi"—eye me derisively and go back to what they were doing: commenting on the merits of passing girls. "Not a bad ass, but the face isn't great," "With a pillow over her head, maybe," "Talk about a draining board!" I get undressed. I have my swimsuit on. My grandmother agreed to stitch foam cups into the top, like the ones she wears since her breast cancer. I just need to be careful to wring them out discreetly when I get out of the water because the foam acts like a sponge, making my fake breasts double in size. The boys have stopped their commentary for now. I can feel their eyes on my back as I walk down to the water. Shame has already given away to something else, I walk with more confidence; in my sister's copy of Charlie Hebdo, all the girls drawn by Wolinski have Fattas. What if it was actually an asset? I swing my hips slightly, to see. The sun warms every part of me in my burning longing to be attractive, to be attractive to them.

Franck is first on the attack. I like his green eyes and shiny brown hair, I think he's manly (boys are dark-haired, girls blond)—the word "manly" makes me shiver, I use it all the time inside my head. We kiss on the beach for two days. On the third day the whole gang goes to the movies. Franck lets the others sit between us, I get the feeling he's deliberately sitting on one end of the row when I'm at the other end next to Hervé. I like Hervé. He's not handsome but he plays the guitar really well, he even has a band in Rouen. Halfway through the film he takes my hand and I interlace my fingers with his. We kiss, he strokes my shoulder, then my thighs, I feel like a guitar. A little later I see him lean to the left, nod his head, and give Franck a thumbs-up in the darkness. Okay fine...the next day I go to see Daniel in his tent, he's reading the civil code in preparation for his first year of law school, he says he finds it relaxing. He's lying down, bare-chested, I put my lips to the curve of his shoulder. We chat for the whole afternoon, he's gentle, funny, intelligent; then we head off to the beach hand in hand. He drinks a lot, which is a shame, he doesn't go anywhere without a can of beer. Drinking is manly, but if you ask me it leaves you in a mess. I sleep with him at night, he strokes my hair, my neck, and my throat. Sometimes when he holds me close I can feel the knife, so hard against my thigh, I break away quickly and he doesn't say anything, or just, "Don't worry." Other times we all play cards together and the other two exchange exasperated glances—it serves them right!

The morning of my last day—the others are staying longer but my father has allowed me only one week's break—Daniel leads me off into the dunes, some way away from the house, it's strange. In a dip in the sand I spot Franck and Hervé looking furious. I turn around but Daniel's disappeared. When I want to go back they catch me by the arms and force me to sit down between them. "So," Franck says, "you thought you could dick us around, did you? Who do you think you are?" "We're not faggots, you know," Hervé joins in, tossing fistfuls of sand at me, "we're not gonna let some girl mess us around like dickheads." I'm not looking at them but scanning the tops of the dunes, did Daniel really abandon me? "I don't think you're dickheads," I say loftily. "Three in one week, isn't that enough? What would you call it?" "I go out with whoever I want, that's all. I do what I want." "Yeah, right, and what you want is to make us look like dickheads." "You're the ones who mistreated me," I say, my face still straining beyond them, my chin tilted up and my neck extended as if I were dancing in *Swan Lake*. "D'you think I didn't see you sending each other signals at the movies? You fell into your own trap, that's what's bugging you." "Stop this holier-than-thou thing," says Franck. "You used us then threw us away and now you're the one complaining!" "Do you know that Prévert poem?" I ask and start reciting:

"I am what I am
I'm made that way.

When I want to have fun
Sure, I laugh and play.
I love whoever loves me.
But is it my fault, say,
if it's not the same guy
that I love every day?

I am what I am
I'm made that way.

What more do you want?
What do you want from me, hey?"

Hervé looks away, the knowing-by-heart must have impressed him. I make the most of this to stand up, there's nothing to add. Franck is furious, he catches me by the ankle. "But that's a whore in your poem! Did you hear that, Hervé, she's reciting a story about a whore! And she's pleased with herself! So we're all agreed here, if you're just a whore, then we can treat you like one. The bar is officially open at Bar-raqué! Help yourselves!" "Stop it," says Hervé, "let her go." "You're chickening out?" Franck snaps. "Don't you want to teach her a lesson, so she learns about life?" My heart starts pounding, it's walking such a thin line, fear is a tightrope walker. Life? But Franck's grip relaxes, I break free and head off with all the dignity that the shaking in my legs will allow. Daniel is sitting in the hollow behind the dune. I walk past him without a word, a princess in her dungeon. He catches up with me: he would never have let them hurt me, he promises, he was waiting for me. "And why did you bring me to them?" (or should I say "summon me"?) I ask, not looking at him but at the sea, the free, wide-open sea. "They just wanted an explanation. I couldn't refuse them that. But they promised me...well, everything's okay, isn't it? I'm here." "You're not my father, you know." (*What an idiot: would my father have any more right?*) "I'm not your father but I'm your boyfriend. We're together, right?" I run down the dune. Learn about life...In the photos that I took along the beach at Coutainville that week, the sand dunes and the small tufts of grass that you walk over in their hollows look a little like women's bodies.

We've now been going out for six months, Daniel wants us to make love but he talks about it rather than doing it. I tell him to wait and he urges me: "When will you want to?" There are two things he doesn't know so we're off to a bad start. First of all, he doesn't know about my father's philosophy, the doctrine about the chestnut...My father wants me to stay a virgin until I'm married, and I obey him. I like obeying. I'm frightened of disobeying. Second, the thing with me is that it's not *wanting* to that I'm waiting for. It's *having* to.

On the insistent recommendation of the teacher's conference, my mother signs me up for a residential language course in London during the Easter vacation. The organization that runs the courses sends me the address of the family I'll be staying with, and I write to them to introduce myself. I reluctantly catch my train on the first day of the Easter break, leaving Daniel to review for his end-of-term exams, and I alight at Waterloo Station with the rest of the group. The English parents are all there at the end of the platform and they step forward toward their guests and exchange a few words before heading for the exit. The platform empties quickly and I'm left all alone with my suitcase at my feet. *How do you do?* I go over and over my first lesson on autopilot, *How do you do?* It's so dumb, it doesn't mean "How are you?" it's not even a complete question: How do you do what? How do I do? How do I do this, alone on a platform at Waterloo Station? I'm fifteen years old and super miserable at a station named after a French defeat. In the end, the organizer comes over with his list and asks my name. "Laurence Barraqué," I say, acutely aware that my first name sounds like *l'eau rance*, foul water, drain water, sewage. He walks along the platform toward an obese couple who look about ready to leave, and comes back to me with them, all smiles. "Peter,

Amy...Laurence." We shake hands obligingly as if passing a sponge to each other. There's been a misunderstanding: "Laurence is a boy's name in English, like the actor Laurence Olivier, you know..." So they were expecting a boy. "I understand," I say. So were my parents, I don't say. "I'm used to it." "But it doesn't matter," the organizer adds, good-naturedly, "a boy or a girl, it's the same."

If you like.

I climb into the back of their car in silence. Peter drives, glancing at me in the rearview mirror with something like amazement. Amy stares at the road ahead. They live in a detached house in the east of the city. Almost before we're in the hall, Amy tilts her face up the stairs and calls ominously, "Helen! Come down! Laurence is here." I put down my suitcase and also look up while syrupy music dribbles down the stairs. A foot in a sequined pump appears on the top step, then another plies through the air, perfectly arched, followed by a leg clothed in black and frothy with frills and lace. A hand with red fingernails strokes the banister rail while, emerging successively from the stairwell with the studied slowness of a headline act, I see a perfectly shaped ass, a narrow waist, creamy breasts offered up like Saint Agatha's on a platter but above a bustier top, a graceful neck, and a smile filled with staggeringly white teeth. At last her face shows itself and its forget-me-not blue eyes whose spark dies the moment they meet mine. "Helen," says her father, gesturing to his daughter who's frozen on the spot, halfway down the stairs, a furious expression on her face. "Laurence is a girl," he declares, half aggrieved and half goading. I give a sketchy greeting with an apology leaking through it, I wish I could get into my suitcase and be sent away, anywhere, but failing that I say, "How do you do?" and give a little curtsey, bending my knee before such beauty: How do you do? How do you get to be so... How do you do it? is more what I mean. After all she's barely any older than I am, she must be seventeen or eighteen, how do you manage to be so beautiful? Helen doesn't reply and goes back up the stairs four at a time. The music is switched off abruptly. She comes back down in jeans and an old T-shirt, and goes to the kitchen to slice carrots. She was hoping for a boy, a French boy, a French lover, and all she gets is me, it's only me.

The things girls do to seduce boys—that's what I discover, and I find it alarming and disturbing. The dresses, the rhinestones, the lipstick... The whole performance... As a girl, I've never done it and it's never been intended for me. Mom doesn't like me copying her, and Dad even less so—Claude wore blush once and he asked her if she wanted to be a clown when she grew up. So why am I so struck, so excited, so intrigued by the charm that it operates? And what about boys, what do they do to seduce us? I think about it, but can find nothing. They're allowed to be themselves, they're confident they'll be loved for who they are, without artifice. So am I really a girl? I don't have varnish on my toenails or makeup, and I hate the thought of shaving my armpits—boys don't do it, neither does my mother, but Helen does, I think she even puts glittery powder there. After my shower in the morning, in the bathroom's wan neon light, I slick back my hair, harden my jaw, and right there, with my bushy eyebrows and unadorned skin, I could be mistaken for my father, there's some boy in my face. I don't know what to think.

My bedroom is across the landing from Helen's. For the whole time I'm in their house, I listen for her comings and goings, I watch her come home drunk some evenings, in a miniskirt and a skimpy tank top. It's only twelve degrees outside but English girls would rather catch cold than sacrifice their low necklines. I find all this dressing up disgusting, but at the same time I long to measure up to it, to be the boy she was expecting. I'm not allowed to have sex with a boy, but there's nothing explicit in the chestnut philosophy on the subject of "going with" your own kind. I don't dare to discuss it with her, my English is too unreliable. I wish we could talk things over. "Why aren't you a boy?" "I'm sorry, I'll change, I promise."

The day before I leave, I give Helen a golden bracelet that I spent hours choosing—I so desperately wanted to please her and for her to kiss me and forgive me. But Helen continues to ignore me—I'm a girl and that's unforgivable.

I leave feeling despised and disappointed. For two weeks in London I was secretly a boy. Laurence. Beefy to go with his family name, and flat-chested. An invisible boy within a girl with no laurels. A loser. Laurence, laureate of nothing at all.

A few weeks later, the student who gives me math lessons in her college dorm will suddenly peel off her Indian tunic halfway through a probabilities question, take my hands, and put them over her breasts. I will dig the tips of my fingers into them, they'll be squishy and warm, lumps of melting butter. "Hey, stop that!" she'll squeal irritably half a minute later. "That's not stroking, that's palpation. Is this a medical checkup or something?" "I'm sorry," I'll say, putting my things in my bag. "I'm sorry, I don't like girls." "You don't like girls," she'll keep saying, even out onto the stairs where I'm making my getaway (*I'll get a terrible grade in math*), "you don't like girls? But you ARE a girl," she calls after me in a strangulated voice.

When I arrive home from London, Daniel tells me he's now with Karine, a first-year student who smokes joints and doesn't play the virgin card. A whore, then, I think to myself. An easy girl, as Nana used to say (I'm a difficult girl). My father hurls the same judgment at my sister one lunchtime, "My daughter's a whore!" right in the middle of our favorite TV game show ("What is the motto of the city of Paris?"), because he found a murky condom floating in the toilet bowl ("*Fluctuat nec mergitur,*" the game-show host tells the uneducated contestant). "No, I'm not," she snarls, jumping to her feet, "I don't take money for it." He also stands, his chin quivering, and he slaps her. I see my sister's cheek flush scarlet, she runs out of the room and Mom goes after her, throwing down her napkin into my father's plate; I want to leave too. "Stay there," says my father. "I forbid you to move."

I sit back down.

Three months later I will make love for the first time on my dentist Dr. Galiot's reclining chair while his whole family is asleep upstairs. Walking along the street, I happen to bump into Jérôme, my not-twin from Sainte-Agathe clinic, the irritating weakling from middle school. It's July and he's wearing a white tank top, he must be around six two and I remember that his mother started him in judo classes in eighth grade because it's "a good sport for calming boys down," the dentist reported to my mother, as he drilled into my teeth without an anesthetic. "Oh, will you stop making such a fuss," he said, turning his attention to me, "you're a big girl now, it won't hurt much and won't last long, and anyway, I'm sure it's not even hurting... It just won't keep its mouth open," he added for the benefit of no one in particular. It's nighttime now, and I'm only bleeding a tiny amount onto the single-use paper hastily rolled out over the chair, it doesn't hurt much and doesn't last long, not long at all even. In the half-light and the smell of bleach, with one arm flung out over the cuspidor, it's the drill's metallic silhouette, its insect legs, and the bumpy surface of Jérôme's back under my other hand that blow me away—and yes, also probably the memory of the ice-cold implement that his father used to put between my jaws to keep them open.

Dad didn't hear the chestnut explode and wants to protect me from my sister's depravity, so he steps up his precautions. I travel for many kilometers on a little scooter with a prescription in Claude's name to buy the contraceptive pill from a pharmacist who won't recognize the name Barraqué. Claude has passed her end-of-school exams and is going off to Canada to follow any career path so long as it gets her away from Rouen. "When will you come back?" "Never."

I join the theater club at high school, I'd like to play Roxane or Bérénice but end up as Agnès in *The School for Wives*. The teacher's pleased. "You're better than the real thing as an ingenue," he tells me with a note of irony as he watches how eagerly I wait for Horace on my cardboard-cutout balcony. He doesn't know that it's at least three years since his ingenue read *The School for Girls*, France's first licentious novel published in 1655, in which the innocent heroine, unlike Agnès, soon knows everything there is to know about "this contraption with which boys pee, which goes by the name of phallus, and is sometimes known as a member, a shaft, a spindle, a dagger, or a love spear." I'm taken with "love spear," I find it touching, the combination of tender emotion and warlike dominion is a sort of conflicted ideal, even though "shaft" is more immediately effective in producing a state of humiliated arousal—the shaft of a knife, the shaft of dentist's drill, the shaft of a spade.

Meanwhile, Jérôme wants us to get married someday. I'm the love of his life, he tells me, the woman of his dreams. It's the first time I've been a woman in a man's opinion, it's too soon, I still feel like a girl, like a daughter rather than a daughter-in-law, especially not my dentist's. "I've loved you ever since I first saw you in the schoolyard at the start of sixth grade. Did you know I chose Russian as my second language just to be in the same class as you in eighth grade?" "No! But why did you always give me such a hard time, then? I hated you. You pulled my braid, you jostled me in the canteen, and you always said the dumbest things. You tripped me up in recess one time and I had three stitches on my knee." "Yes, I know. It's because I was in love." He'd like to have three children, a boy and two girls if possible, but he's fine with anything. "They'll be so cute!" he exclaims, his naked body intertwined with mine. "I can picture them already!" He has some ideas for a house, he's drawing plans, could easily see himself as an architect. "Look," he shows me one drawing, "we'll have a games room here with a Ping-Pong table, a foosball table, and a little puppet theater. You can write the plays and we'll perform them for our kids." I can't believe the way he says "our kids," he's almost shaking at the thought. I get the feeling that what he's hoping more than anything else is that he'll have me completely to himself and I won't ever be able to get away. Being a mother is definitive. But I'm seventeen with waist-length hair and entirely different games rooms. At high school the boys play baseball with their shirts off in the yard; when they shoot, the muscles in their arms harden under their tan skin, sweat makes their shoulders gleam like apples you want to bite into, and when they score they dispense a round of back slaps and triumphant smiles. Their power, their skin and sheer beauty keep my nose pressed to the window, "Barraqué, please, could you come back and join us?" The young leads in the theater club are through with skin breakouts, some are growing beards. And this kitten's now a full-grown pussycat. "Ah, yes, Molière. Good, great," my father says approvingly. "Let's just see each other tomorrow," I tell Jérôme who wants to walk me home, "I'm going to the library, I have an essay to hand in." In the common room people are preparing for the next high-school party. Lights blaze and the chestnut season is in full swing.

I couldn't really say when it malfunctioned—was it when I threw up my sangria after my mock exams, or when I gave my cousin my blister pack of pills?—but here are the facts: I'm late. Very late, even. The test that I do at dawn in the bathroom confirms things—oh, the terror of running into my father as I emerge from there ashen—and a rapid calculation confirms: I'm also very behind schedule to resolve the problem displayed in two colored lines on the strip. Simone Veil's law was passed less than two years ago but it can't be done here in Rouen where every doctor knows my name. I call Daniel, he's pursuing his studies in Paris, we haven't seen each other in forever but who cares, he's studying law, he'll tell me who to contact in this emergency.

He's so kind over the phone and suggests I should make an appointment with the MLAC. "The MLAC?" "Yes it's a movement for freedom of access to abortion and contraception. You can come to my apartment if you want. I'm near Montparnasse." He's still with Karine but they don't live together, their role models are Sartre and Beauvoir, he explains. The "contingent" and the "necessary" and all that. "Aha," I say. Paris changes people so much, he seems confident and sure of himself. As for me, I've been to Paris only five or six times in my life even though Rouen is just eighty minutes from Gare Saint-Lazare. One time, when I was seven, I went to the Opéra with my grandparents. Another time I went to a car show with my father. Apart from that, I mostly know the Gare de Lyon from our train journeys to La Chaux for the summer vacation.

The woman who sees me at the MLAC doesn't look very understanding. She can't be more than forty years old but because she's not wearing a jot of makeup, she looks older than my mother. When she starts talking, though, her soft voice reassures me. She explains how the procedure will work if I go to the address she's about to give me. While she talks me through the various stages, she takes a transparent cannula from a drawer. I'm not listening. I don't want to know, I just want it to be over. To the right of her desk there's a banner on the wall with large letters in black masking tape, some of them peeling off. It reads: MY BODY BELONGS TO ME. "But I see that you're not yet eighteen," she says. "That's a problem. You'll need your parents' consent." I blench. "No, no, that's not possible." "Not even your mother?" she asks. I shake my head, the truth is I haven't even thought of this, it hasn't occurred to me to discuss the situation with her. "You know, in my experience, mothers are often more understanding than you'd think. Yours is from the generation who knew about backstreet abortions, that does help. I'll give you the form to fill out. Talk to her about it. Just one signature is enough." "Thank you. I'll do that."

The doctor whose contact details I've been given at the Clinique des Ternes is an intern just finishing his specialty in obstetrics and gynecology. I hand him the form on which I've forged my mother's signature. I was tempted to put both signatures but my hand shook too much with my father's, I was frightened of betraying him. The intern explains everything again, punctuating his sentences with "Do you understand?" and makes an appointment for me after the seven-day thinking time stipulated by the law. "It gives you an opportunity to reach this decision perfectly calmly. Do you see?" "Yes." "Have you discussed this with the father?" "The father?" "Yes, the child's father. Do you not have any alternatives?" "No."

My only alternative is between Jérôme and Mikis, a Greek boy on a language-exchange program at high school. But don't let's go into details.

"So there's one thing that's bothering me," I tell Daniel who's sitting cross-legged on his studio's carpeted floor, with a joint in his mouth as he takes the cap off a beer. "He asked me if I'd talked to 'the child's father.'" "Yeah?" Daniel manages. "It's the fact that he used the word 'child,' you see, it seemed weird." "Well, it's stupid to say that before a termination. Because there is no child, that's the whole point. And so there are no parents." I don't know why but I don't like Daniel's reaction. But I keep going: "But what's even weirder is I also find it kind of reassuring, this feeling that I have or I'm harboring a child, well, a baby in the making. I don't know why, it's a confidence boost. I feel, how can I put this? Powerful...but at the same time I don't want children, I don't think I'll ever have any." "Why?" "I don't know. I want to be free. To keep acting, to write a play, I don't know, live my life." I can tell that

Daniel is moved by this. It occurs to me that in the end we never made love. But now's not the time. Let's change the subject. "These feminists, the MLAC? Do you know them? They gave me brochures for the MLF, the women's liberation movement. I think—after all this—I'll join them, we need to show solidarity, girls supporting girls." "Yes, the MLAC's a good thing, it's radical. But now that you've secured the right to have abortions, contraception, and everything, you need to calm down. Enough already with burning your bras and declaring war on men. The aim now should be understanding and harmony between the sexes." "Yes, well, men *are* still more powerful, they instinctively want to dominate. And we girls take the flak. I mean, when I go out late, even in Rouen, I'm scared on the streets. I've gotten into the habit of carrying keys between my fingers, like brass knuckles. You don't do stuff like that, you guys..." "No," Daniel concedes. "But men are scared too, you know, don't go thinking they're not. When it comes to fear, we're equals. Even in elementary school we're scared of not being good enough. We have to be on our guard the whole time, we have to fight and not cry and impress the girls. We're scared we won't be brave enough, scared we'll have to fight to show who's the strongest, and scared it won't be us. When we grow up, we're scared we won't get an erection when we need one, scared we won't handle stuff, scared of being humiliated. No, seriously, it's really tough being a boy."

During my seven-day thinking time back in Rouen, I borrow books about feminism from the library. I spend whole afternoons lying around, reading in my nightdress on the living-room sofa. "Get off your ass a bit, anyone would think you're pregnant," my mother jokes. I keep my eyes focused on the page. The activists from the early days—barely more than five or six years ago—witnessed violent reactions: physical and verbal abuse, threats at work, at home, and in society at large. They were called bitches, dykes, and sex-starved. "What's the difference between a woman and a horse?" asks a passerby in news coverage of an MLF demonstration. "There's no difference: you just need to know how to ride them." I recognize the dad-style humor and it suddenly strikes me as leaden, but I still smile.

I haven't opted for a general anesthetic, first of all, because I want to be able to leave the clinic the same day, then, because it's a little less expensive (Daniel's loaning me the money), and last, because I don't like the idea of not being there, not being me (what if I died during the operation?). "This is going to hurt," the doctor warns me. "The pain is similar to childbirth. Which doesn't mean much to you, I know. Or me, for that matter." Whether you're bringing a life into the world or snuffing one out, the pain's the same, I think to myself with no sense of surprise. A balancing payment for being alone.

While he prepares his instruments, the doctor asks me what I'm studying. With my feet up in stirrups, I tell him that after my end-of-school exam I'm planning to start a course at the school of Oriental languages with a view to becoming an interpreter. I also say I'm passionate about theater and have played a part in Molière's *The School for Wives*, I start telling him about the role of Agnès in case his memories of his schooldays are hazy. "But actually," I say, warming to my theme, "what I really wa—" "Okay, stop talking now," he interrupts me, "I'm starting the procedure." I hold my tongue, ashamed of my tide of words: I always have to show off, don't I?

Afterward I spend a few hours lying on a bed surrounded by other women who've just had abortions. Two of them are crying. The nurse takes care of them, then the doctor comes and sits on the edge of their beds, comforts them, and tries to make them laugh. I myself don't have any particularly strong emotions, I'm empty of feelings: devoid of thoughts and pain. They ask me if someone's coming to collect me and I say yes. Almost before I'm out the door I light a cigarette, and I walk along the street smoking. Even in Paris women give me sideways glances. In the packed Métro taking me back to Daniel's place where I'm to spend the night, I like the anonymity of the crowd. What happened? Nothing. I'm an abstract entity among many others. All these bodies tight up against each other are just one compact and indifferent block. Object lesson: Oblivion.

Daniel presses the buzzer to open the door and asks "Are you okay?" over the intercom. I climb the three floors and go into his apartment; he's listening to Jefferson Airplane, "*Don't you want somebody to love, don't you need somebody to love.*" "Nostalgia, nostalgia," I say, taking off my coat. I hang it on the hook and in the half-light of the corridor I notice a dribble of white trickling down to the hem. I put my hand on it and snatch it away immediately. It's semen.

two

"*It's a boy.*

"There. Look. Can you see?"

You can see. You're hypnotized by that small squiggle between the thighs on the glowing screen. Yes, you can see
something. There's something there. Straining toward
the screen, your husband, Christian, has tears in his eyes,
he looks proud—of himself more than of you, if you look
closely, but you're not looking. Besides, the same can be
said of you: you can't get over it, you have a *boy* inside you.
That word is your triumphant achievement. You have built
a gender that isn't your own, you're powerful, it's incredible, you have to see it to believe it. Your sister, Claude,

has two girls, her husband already had a boy but that's not the same—an honorary son—and anyway, they live in Canada and never come back. You meanwhile are in Rouen, you'll give birth in the city where you were born. That will make your father happy, you instantly think of him, of his dream that you're finally realizing, only at one step removed: though not the father of a boy, he'll be grandfather to one; you're giving him a grandson, offering him a boy baby doll. You picture the day he'll hold him in his arms. He's kept the race-car circuit from your childhood, you know he has, you've seen it on top of the cupboard in the garage, you couldn't believe your eyes, after all this time! He even took it with them when they moved. He'll be able to get it down now, put batteries into it again, and set it out on the living-room carpet. You're going to make your father happy—none too soon.

He is happy. He looks at the scan photo you show him and winks: "I knew you had balls, my girl." Everyone laughs. The paradox is intoxicating, and who cares if you're not the first. You're expecting a boy: a happy event. You feel invincible, you thrust out your stomach importantly, Big Belly now earns nothing but respect. "I warn you," Christian jokes when you're alone together, "that it's actually thanks to me." And he shows me a page from *Parents* magazine that he tore out in the waiting room: "The quality of sexual intercourse also affects the baby's sex. A woman's orgasm produces many contractions in the vagina, allowing the faster male sperm cells to reach the ovum even more quickly. Conversely, the absence of a female orgasm favors the conception of a girl." "So who do we thank?" You both laugh, ha ha, boys run faster than girls, you lean into him tenderly: "Well, obviously it's your doing, my love." (With an unpaid contribution from the forty thieves whom you imagined taking you by force in Ali Baba's cave, but you abstain from associating them with this shared happiness.)

Against all expectations—no one understands the mysteries of a marriage—your parents are still together. André decided to stay with his wife when she had their second son, your father likes your mother's cooking, and she simply renewed any marriage vows on the condition that they bought twin beds. "You must be happy to be having a boy," your father says to Christian. Your mother mitigates: "What really matters is that everything goes well. Having a girl is nice too. And here's proof," she says, patting your arm. "My two girls are the best things I did in life." She seems a little absent, perhaps she's remembering Gaëlle. You, though, are thinking about the clinic in Ternes a long time ago, when you didn't want a child. In the early years you often wondered whether it had been a boy or a girl. But you never wanted to imagine its face or furnish it with a life. And now you can forget it. You're married, your name's no longer Barraqué but Charpentier, Laurence Charpentier. Fate has a teasing sense of humor: Charpentier means carpenter, a good solid name, but it's the masculine form of the word—like being called Goodman, Freeman, or Coleman—and this always sounds a false note to you, leaving you feeling out of step or indecisive because you can never make the genders in your name agree. (Although the feminine version, Charpentière, doesn't even exist, and who ever heard of a Goodwoman or a Colewoman?) You met Christian at a party in Paris, he's an engineer, he went to the prestigious Ponts et Chaussées civil engineering school like your grandfather, he plays tennis as your mother once did, and he has just secured his pilot's license at Rouen airfield. Although he's a scientist, he managed to recite a Ronsard poem to you that first evening, *Mignonne, allons voir si la rose*, and you liked that... You yourself rather rushed into it and you sometimes jokingly explain that this was to honor the promise you made to Nana to get married before you turned twenty-five. You laugh, but sadly it's true: you were married two weeks before your twenty-fifth birthday, to avoid being an "old maid." After you were married, you and Christian spent a few years traveling, having fun, and not feeling the need to start a family. When you were studying languages, you tried to write a play and even a novel, but eventually gave up, thinking you didn't have enough talent or rather that your talent lay in being at the service of other people's talent. Christian is tall, dark, and manly, he's four years older than you are and you love him. You get along well and rarely argue. Just one time he slapped you hard enough to knock your head off; as you felt your brain rattle inside your skull you thought it was all over between you. You had a detached retina and needed laser surgery. The neck pain took longer to wear off. But you forgave him, and anyway, you'd slightly gotten what you deserved—you'd been delving through his wallet to stoke your jealousy. The two of you came back to live in Rouen shortly after you finished your degree, life isn't as expensive as in Paris and your husband likes knowing you're near your parents when he's traveling. If you thought about it, you'd realize you have exactly the sort of life Jérôme once talked about and that you scoffingly deemed so humdrum. You're a trilingual interpreter and translator—you and Christian have decided that you'll now work mainly on translation to avoid traveling and so that you can devote yourself to the baby, your son, your firstborn.

Dr. Dubecq, your gynecologist, would have been happier if you hadn't asked to know the baby's sex when you had the five-month scan. In her experience, when the sex doesn't coincide with the parents' hopes, the birth is more difficult, often requiring an epidural, even a cesarean, as if there were some subconscious reticence. But in this case, well, it worked out fine, you got what you wanted. In fact, you hadn't expressed a particular preference; after wavering for a while, you hadn't even adopted a recommended diet for choosing the baby's sex. So over the ensuing weeks she needn't hold back in describing the baby's growth. "Well, my friend, this one's going to be a rugby prop," she says, and you can't help smiling, you're not surprised, only sorry you no longer have your grandfather to tell. Yes, he'll play rugby, you silently promise yourself, but he'll be a winger, like his great-grandfather, it's not as dangerous as prop. Christian, on the other hand, would prefer his son to take up boxing, he can picture the two of them swinging at the punching bag he's hung from the garage ceiling; he's tall handsome and agile, and when he steps into the ring he already has the beginnings of a mustache. And he'll fly too, of course. It only remains to find a first name for this copilot. You both start talking to him, leaning an ear to your stomach to see what he thinks—Tristan? Gabriel? Nicholas?—and he replies in Morse code like in the Tintin adventure *The Shooting Star*, never saying the same thing twice. The three of you huddle around your navel, rabbits playing the tom-tom in a children's picture book. "Gabriel won't work," your husband says one day. "If it was girl, fine: Gabrielle with two l's." It takes you a moment to hear what he did, you're just registering that l sounds like *aile*—the word for wing—when he concludes that "it's impossible for an aviator to have only one *aile*." You laugh—an aviator with only one wing! "Very true," you say. And the same goes for Gaël, you think. Without daring to admit it, you secretly don't want a mixed-sex name.

You can hear the feminine pronoun *elle* in the French pronunciation of Gabriel. You want a virile name or, better still, one that doesn't have a girl's version—Jérôme, Thierry, Bruno, Arthur...to make things clear. "You're crazy, you're son's making you crazy," says Christian and you just love it when he says "your son."

You're seven months pregnant when your parents come to see you, they have something important to tell you. The thing is your father's heard awful rumors about his coworker, your gynecologist Dr. Dubecq. She's apparently come to work at the clinic drunk several times, has been unable to assist births adequately, far less to operate, so another specialist had to take over in an emergency, besides, at barely forty, she's not very experienced, she might lose her nerve, and it would only need to be her time of the month and, well, "this Dubecq stinks," he says. Your face is ghostly pale, you don't feel like laughing. What to do? You've always been pleased with your gynecologist, even if you have known her only three years. She's attentive, she's understanding, she sometimes calls you "my friend." Before her, you were with Dr. Bonnard but he died of a heart attack like your grandfather, aged sixty-three. He was an unusual kind of doctor, it was as if he'd never managed to shake off his med-school mentality, he'd never let you leave without telling you a lewd joke, and you laughed, perhaps because he reminded you of your father. He was also a sexologist and advocated sexual pleasure to help relationships thrive, as indicated in the brochures laid out on his desk. His secretary was his wife, a sour woman who was a poor advertisement for his therapeutic competence. You were careful not to consult him on the subject, even if he encouraged you to, probing you to find out whether you were *kind* to your husband, whether you *made an effort*. You didn't reply, but you didn't stop him either. "Have you heard the one about the two blondes coming out of a nightclub in the middle of nowhere? They're drunk and far from home and they don't have anyone to drive them back so they start walking along the road. One of them suddenly stops, realizing her friend's no longer with her. She searches for her in the darkness and eventually sees her in a field, kneeling next to a cow and diligently sucking one of its teats. 'What the hell are you doing?' asks the first one. 'Look, I'm done with walking,' says her friend, 'and one of these four is bound to have a car.'" You laughed only to make him happy, because you'd gotten into the habit of making people happy and you were waiting for your prescription. One time, he hadn't had the results back from your tests so he called the laboratory and, while waiting for a reply he looked at you where he'd pinioned you into position with your legs splayed under the surgical light. "Okay, so what am I supposed to do now, I've got my patient waiting with a speculum up her rear end!" he roared into the mouthpiece with little attention to anatomical accuracy. "Yes, yes, the courier, fine, he'll be here in five minutes, but what are we going to do to pass the time?" and he turned to wink at you. You smiled feebly. You weren't displeased when a woman took over his office, and you didn't feel you had to collude with her. And now you have to change again, and while you're pregnant? What if that's bad luck? You've been beset with superstitions since the start of this pregnancy.

"Luckily, I have a solution," says your father, taking your hand. "Sit down and I'll explain." You sit down and withdraw your hand—you love your father but don't like him touching you. The very sight of blotchy skin appalls you, you clench your teeth and your legs. This disgust is instinctive, like your terror of cockroaches and spiders, you can hide it but you still feel it, and you have to avert your eyes from age spots, which your grandmother used to call cemetery flowers—if you look at them you're the one who dies, it's your coffin that they're strewn over. Your father, it turns out, has found a substitute: Dr. Guerry. Charles Guerry. Is this a joke? The man's name sounds like *guéri*—healed, cured, all better now. "It was his vocation, as you can see, with that reassuring name, even though pregnancy's not an illness, my darling," your mother adds. Your parents are good friends with his father, Robert Guerry, who has now retired but was an obstetrician at Sainte-Agathe for many years. And they know Charles well too, because your father took him as a locum tenens at his office several times when he was away for vacations—a remarkable fellow, formerly an intern in hospitals in Lille but he's moved back to Rouen to take over from his father . . . to make a long story short, the boy's brilliant, they conclude, yes, a remarkable boy. "You'll be completely safe with him, you can do it with your eyes closed," says your father. "And I'm sure you'll notice," your mother chips in, "he's a good-looking boy. That never does any harm."

It comes as a painful surprise, when you're more than seven months pregnant, to have to meet an obstetrician you've never seen before—and what lie will you serve up to your existing gynecologist? But do you have any choice?

On first meeting, Dr. Charles Guerry is the cold, haughty type, though this is tempered by the fact that you're Dr. Barraqué's daughter. That doesn't stop you being a nulliparous ignoramus, and a tiresome one with your anxious questions: The baby isn't too big, is he? Will I need a cesarean? How does an epidural work? First of all, it's not the fetus that's too big but you. It's time you went on a diet. Secondly, cesareans are for losers and for lazy doctors who want to head off on their vacations. He, well *he*'s brought much bigger babies than yours into the world by the natural route. Nature is the only thing that's real, and women have a tendency to forget that. The same goes for pain, it's natural. Which is why he personally is loath to suggest an epidural, which—incidentally—disappoints a lot of laboring women: do you really want to miss the best day of your life? Women usually regret it: after all, they won't have that many other opportunities in their lives to show a bit of courage, wouldn't you agree?

"He said 'the fetus.'" That evening on the phone you're almost in tears. "I said 'the baby' and he corrected me." Your father is irritated: "Oh, you women like to play this your own way! When you want abortions, the word fetus suits you just fine. Embryo, egg, you're happy with anything. And then bam! All of a sudden it's a baby." When he hears you sniffling nervously he calms down—a pregnant woman is more vulnerable than your everyday woman, med students learn that from their first-year textbook. "I'll explain, Laurence," he says with a smile in his voice. "Fetus is the accurate term, it's the technical term. It shocks you because you're not a scientist, but it's normal coming from a conscientious practitioner."

You go shopping with your mother and buy pale blue wool to make baby clothes and she gives you a white sleepsuit. "You know," she says thoughtfully while you're waiting patiently at the checkout, "I sometimes think everything would have been so much easier if I'd had a boy. Your father would have been so happy, so happy...Maybe he would have loved me more, with a boy. Definitely."

You have violent contractions more than two weeks before you're due, a pale liquid trickles down your legs. Christian is on a business trip in Chicago until the end of the week. It's seven in the morning, the sun isn't up yet. You call your mother who takes you to Sainte-Agathe clinic where you were born thirty-five years ago. "Oh, I don't like this place," says your mother as you walk into the entrance hall. You're hot and you're frightened, you don't belong in any happy memories, but you're only thinking about one thing: the date. The day of your son's birthday. Today. My son, you keep saying, cradling the word in the echo chamber of your head. My son. It feels so strange uttering something you've never said before. Words are newborn too.

You're hot because you have a temperature of 102. You're baby's heart beats on the monitor, which reassures you because you haven't felt him move for two or three days. "It's because he's big, he's run out of room," your father explained. The Sainte-Agathe midwives are secular these days—Sister Catherine, who brought you into the world, died a long time ago. They no longer wear wimples but pink nurse's caps, they're all coming and going because it's handover time to the day shift. You're settled into a delivery room and your mother goes downstairs to fill in forms and call your husband. You're left on your own. Chicago–Rouen, that's a long way, Christian won't be here in time. You're in pain, and now can't remember whether you settled on Gilles or Arthur before he left.

Meanwhile the midwife from the day shift lets Dr. Guerry know that you have a temperature, probably an infection, she'll wait for his instructions. "I'm on my way," he says.

The truth is that Dr. Guerry is still in bed and this information annoys him. It's Monday, and if you'd had the good sense to go into labor the day before, he wouldn't have had to make a decision, he wasn't on duty. Now, though, he can hear a note of urgency in Roselyne the midwife's voice. He doesn't like that, it's unusual for her. He doesn't like making decisions, he's not used to it. He became a doctor because his father pushed him into it; he'd dreamed of traveling far and wide, gathering plants and creating perfumes. As a child, he picked flowers in the garden and crushed them with herbs to alter their fragrance, then he would daub his concoction on his mother's neck. And now he must go back, yet again, to the smell of blood and shit and ether that shrouds his life. So he gets up, sets the coffee maker going, turns on the radio, listens to the news, then the weather—it's going to snow in Normandy—and butters a third slice of toast. Then he takes a long shower, dresses, hesitates between several different ties, and calls back his ex-wife who left him a very curt message about her alimony. On his first day at med school fifteen years ago, Professor Gaubert, a bigwig who was a friend of his father's, had started his speech like this: "Good morning, all of you. Today you're embarking on a long journey to realize your dearest wishes. As you well know, the selection process is tough and I'd like to give you the latest statistics: only fourteen percent of students here in this amphitheater will become doctors. But I can reassure the ladies present—with a little perseverance, more than fifty percent of you will become female doctors." Everyone laughed, except for a few crosspatches. But Charles should have listened to the message, he's paying heavily for this lack of perspicuity now. If he could do this without harming his career, he'd admit that he doesn't much like women. He doesn't understand them. What do they want? Love, money, security, sex, adventure? It's still an enigma, but he has no desire to play that detective. He sometimes even feels nauseous when confronted with their stretch marks and their purplish mucous surfaces, and there's no one to confess this to.

Yesterday, like every Sunday, he went to mass with his mother before Sunday lunch in the family home—his mother wears Guerlain's Shalimar, with not entirely the right amount of discretion for a church service, he thought. His father asked him how he was settling in at Sainte-Agathe—he's only been working there a few months—and segued into his perennial guidance drawn from his own experience, stroking the small Légion d'honneur medal on his lapel all the while. What angers Dr. Guerry senior is the incompetence of young doctors, always more preoccupied with paying off their loans than learning their trade. But what finer vocation can there be than the giving of life? He was instrumental in pointing his son, Charles, toward this career path and then recommended him to the clinic. The boy is slightly timorous but he'll make a niche for himself in the end. His daughter followed in his footsteps too, she's a nurse and she married a cardiologist. No, young doctors these days have no balls, he railed not for the first time, they go along with all the latest fads, cesareans and epidurals left, right, and center. "You won't go in for all that, will you, Charles?" he asked, helping himself to more roast lamb. "Well done, Anne-Sophie, this slow-cooked joint is wonderful." His wife smiled and made a sign of the cross on the bread.

Charles Guerry drives into the clinic's parking lot at ten o'clock. He goes upstairs, puts on his lab coat, says hello to some midwives in the corridor, then makes up his mind to visit the only newly delivered mother and lingers at her bedside making jokes. She wants a photo of herself with him and her baby who popped out as if she'd been shelling peas the week before with no need for his intervention, so he poses graciously with a smile on his lips, willingly taking on the role of the grateful father he isn't.

He finally comes into your delivery room looking busy with his lab coat open as if gusted by the wind to reveal a gray suit. It's ten thirty. You've been here for three hours and you're dripping with sweat, but you haven't dared complain or ask for water, you don't want to be any trouble. You should have asked, that's what the midwives are here for, he explains. He gets you to put your feet in stirrups, examines you, and peers at the curved surface of the monitor. Behind him, the midwife Roselyne gives you an anxious smile. "Should I give her antibiotics?" she suggests. "Let's see," he replies. "It's going to have to be a section, isn't it?" she continues. "Perhaps. Let's see." "But..." she ventures. He eyes her scornfully and leaves the room. You're frightened and in pain but now's not the time to make a fuss; and besides, you have faith in this brilliant boy, you're having a brilliant boy yourself and his heart is pounding away on the screen smeared with fingerprints. Your mother's left, she'll be told when it's time. Over in Chicago, Christian's trying to find a flight.

The doctor comes back at midday. You're suffering with all your might, enduring a mother's noble pain, which is mangling your insides, but what you'd like, actually, if possible, without meaning to complain or be pushy, what you'd like is to have an epidural. He waves the idea away while you're talking: No, no, come on, that's not an option, you'd be risking an infection, and anyway you don't have much longer now, your cervix is fully dilated, the fetus's head is almost engaged, which, incidentally, is why a cesarean is no longer a possibility either. A bit of spirit! A bit of patience! You'll have a vaginal delivery within an hour, something to show for your labors.

You give birth three hours later in the company of the midwife and three men whose role you don't know, they weren't introduced to you but stand in a circle around your gaping vagina. One is wearing a bow tie, he looks ridiculous, you think between pushes. "Go on, your hands are smaller," the doctor suddenly tells Roselyne, stepping aside from between your legs to make way for her. Why would anyone become an obstetrician if their hands were too big? The question evaporates: your poorly oxygenated brain is dissolving the world. In the end, just when you're about to pass out (there's a sudden darkness), you feel your baby's body stretching endlessly out of you without a sound, you mold every detail of him, his head, his legs, his heels. Your son. A dress that you saw in a magazine, pink with lace on the sleeves, keeps you on the right side of consciousness, as if it were there on a hanger: you'll look gorgeous in it with your baby in your arms in a blue romper suit made of soft wool. You'll send everyone this picture of the two of you to announce his arrival.

While you've been admiring yourself in the pink dress everyone else has left, as if fleeing the room. Not a word was exchanged. You come back to your senses. You're alone and you can't hear anything, isn't it odd that your baby's not on your chest crying? Aren't they normally put straight onto the mother's breasts? Or has everyone gone off to clean him up and take his measurements? You don't know, it's your first baby. Your mother never described it. Your exhausted body strains to hear a cry, but there's nothing. No one. Boys don't cry, you remember, perhaps that's why you can't hear anything.

The baby's hardly extricated, passed from the midwife's hands to the pediatricians, and Dr. Guerry's no longer sure what to do. If he listened to his heart, he'd go home. Now, once again, there's nothing to decide, the future is no longer his responsibility. He shuts himself in his office, sniffs the tube of peppermint spirit that always lives in his drawer, and calls his father. "Yes, a drag, a birth that went badly…no, no, couldn't possibly have predicted it, a real shit show: shoulders obstructing, fetal distress, anoxia. No, he's not dead, the pediatrician took care of him, but his Apgar score's very low. We called an ambulance. What? The mother? How do you mean, the mother? She's Dr. Barraqué's daughter, you know, the GP I used to locum for. Yes, yes, of course, I'm going, I'll call you back. Excuse me? Primipara. Thirty-five. Yes, you're right, I'll do that, good idea."

He comes back. The delivery room is empty, there's just you, awash with sweat and blood. Had he forgotten you? You ask how your baby's doing, why he didn't cry, he tells you the baby's being taken care of, and you'll see him soon. Roselyne puts her head around the door, she looks wrung out with dark rings under her eyes and an evasive expression, and she slips away again as soon as she's whispered hastily in the doctor's ear. "I'm going to stitch

you back up," he announces. With his impassive face between your legs, he mournfully pulls the needle. Just for
a moment, this familiar gesture reassures you, it reminds
you of your great-grandmother, her face tilted toward the
lamplight. You can't feel anything, no pain, you are re-
duced to sight and hearing, on the lookout, a spotter at a
castle window. You don't exist, you simply listen. A man
is doing some sewing at the far end of your bed. And, on
his father's advice, this man, Dr. Charles Guerry, is giving
you a "husband stitch." He doesn't explain what it is, you
have other fish to fry but there it is: you're very badly torn
so really tightening the vaginal orifice will help your partner resume sexual activity. And you'll be needing it—given
that you're already thirty-five, you mustn't waste time before having more children, do you understand?

You might understand if he explained: he's doing this
for you. There's nothing else he can do for you.

All at once there's a woman in white standing at your
bedside. She introduces herself, she's a pediatrician at
Rouen's general hospital, she's escorting the ambulance
that the clinic called to come and take your baby. She
leans over you as if over a cradle and talks right up next
to you, her face almost touching yours. You see the scatter
of dilated pores on her skin, the bags under her eyes, how
tired she is, and how young. She's squeezing your hand
in one of hers and stroking your forehead with the other,
your hair is plastered with sweat. Her voice is gentle. "I'm

going to take your baby. It's a boy, did you know that? He's not well at all, he took a long time to breathe. We're going to do everything we can to get him back to you soon and in good health. But his chances are slim and I have to tell you that it's possible, it's probable, likely even, that you won't have, well, that there may not be a baby." She's fumbling for words, you indicate with your eyelids that you understand, you treasure the tears in the corners of her eyes, it's the only thing anyone can give you, the gift of tears. She asks you what his name is, you shake your head, you don't know what his name is, will you ever have an opportunity to use it, to call him by his name, you wish she would say yes, oh yes, of course, you'll call out his name and he'll come, he'll run to you from the far end of the yard. She's waiting, you need to be quick, you don't want to give the name that's been chosen, you're casting around for a different name, the name of a different child, not this one, another one, the name of a child who might die. She's waiting, her eyes are sad, she brings her ear up to your mouth which whispers as if betraying a secret, "Tristan, Tristan," you say, "Tristan," she says, gathering in the name and taking it away with her.

Several minutes pass. You're lying in a coffin of time. Then the bow tie comes back. He stands next to you with his hands by his sides like a toy soldier. He gives a sort of click

of his heels—attention!—and says, "The child has died."
You try to meet his eyes, but no. He squeezes your hand
and leaves. You're left alone with those words, learning
them.

The child has died. Who does that mean? It has no name,
no gender, no family ties. Who is it? It's the child you
don't have.

Hours trickle by, thoughts are stupid, quivering, fleeting
things. You're lying on the field of honor on a bloodied
sheet. The forgotten memory of your abortion comes
back to you, that was eighteen years ago, you stayed at the
clinic for two or three hours after the procedure, you were
alone, as you are now, you hadn't even told Jérôme. Shame
and regret grapple with your grief. Your punishment is
disproportionate. "I'm so sorry," says the midwife. "What
happened, my girl?" asks your father, his face unrecognizable. He wants to talk to the obstetrician but the man
has private consultations on Monday afternoons. Your
mother says nothing, she's in a different time zone, there
aren't the words. In the evening a meal is brought to you
on a tray. Ham with pasta shells, your favorite dish when
you were a child. While people talk to you, "You must
eat," your father says decisively, you diligently chop your

food into tiny pieces that spill off the plate, off the tray. You parents exchange anxious looks at the sight of you covering your bed in little morsels.

Your husband comes into the room at last. He is gray, he's shaking. When he takes you in his arms he dissolves into tears, holding you so tightly he chokes you, and you both sob. Then he tears himself away, retreats to a corner of the room and cries on his own, leaning against the wall. You've never seen your husband cry. His pain is so raw that your father goes over and hugs him. "Be brave," he murmurs. And when Christian, who lost his parents young, surrenders to this affectionate gesture from his father-in-law and collapses against him, the older man pats his back, "Be brave, Christian," he says, then, as the sobbing grows louder, he takes his shoulders, "be strong" (and he addresses him in the familiar *tu* form rather than the more formal *vous* for the first time since your marriage), he stands him up tall, "come on, my boy, be brave," holds him up against the wall, "be a man."

You watch them.

People say, "Be a man." No one ever says, "Be a woman."

The following day, at the hospital's suggestion and against Dr. Guerry's advice, you slip out of the clinic for a couple of hours so that you and Christian can visit your son in the morgue in the basement of the university hospital. Almost before you've left the morgue, you want to go back, you want to hold him close one more time, for the last time, and whisper something in his ear, but you're not allowed back in, and you stand there pressed against the glass door through which a member of the staff wags a finger to mean no. Two days later, on the morning of the funeral, you leave the maternity floor for good, a place where you were meant to be resting amid the cries of tiny babies and the laughter of new mothers. "You must *rest*," the doctor said, looking concerned for your health. "You're weak, you shouldn't get out of bed." In the end he's agreed to let you leave, making you fill out a disclaimer which he watched you sign.

Christian hasn't come to pick you up, he's escorting the body, but your parents are waiting in the entrance hall at Sainte-Agathe to take you to the cemetery. They're sitting with their backs to you on plastic chairs and don't hear you arrive. "Poor man, he must feel terrible," your father's saying. You freeze. They're talking about your husband, you think, it's always the same: even now, at a time like this, you come second, you don't count. "Starting out on a career with a tragedy like this, what a shame, such a brilliant boy." "Yes," says your mother, "he so desperately wanted to do well, he pressured himself." "I'll write him a little letter in a couple of weeks. There's no point in him losing sleep, it happens to everyone. He didn't deserve this. And I'll call his father." "Yes," says your mother, "it could help him turn the corner."

You stay there, paralyzed. *It doesn't happen to everyone, it's happening to me. Me. Me, Laurence. Your daughter. I'm the one who needs help. Did I deserve this?* You want to protest but you don't know how to—Protestant is just an empty term inherited from your father, and you haven't been taught to make yourself heard. You back out of the hall with your bag full of blue baby clothes knit by your own hand, the health record book in its blue plastic cover, and the blue baby bracelet with the name Tristan on it. In some cultures death is seen as a woman when it's actually a blue horseman, you know it is, you can just see him galloping on and on, extinguishing the spark in people's eyes.

After the cemetery—where, side by side in little white coffins, Gaëlle and Tristan form an incestuous young couple—you go home. Your husband returned to Chicago straight after the ceremony, it's an important contract, he can't afford to mess it up. When you take a shower that evening you feel a swelling form between your thighs—what could it...?—and with one push you deliver a gelatinous mass that slumps at your feet in the bathtub. You're thrust into a horror film. You scream. You scream but you're alone, no one hears you, no one comes running. You run naked to the phone and stand there shivering as you call your father: he's a doctor, he'll help you. "Calm down, darling," he says, "you're hysterical, I can't understand a word you're saying." You calm down and describe the thing for him, a blood-soaked jellyfish with fringed edges like seaweed. "It must be some of the placenta," you say because you can't imagine what else it could be. "Come on, you're talking nonsense, seriously," your father retorts immediately. "It can't be placenta tissue. That's impossible." "But yes, it is" (you remember an illustration in a book you read while you were pregnant) "and anyway, what else can it be? My womb tumbling out?" You shriek. "Stop it, Laurence, don't be stupid. You don't know anything about all this for goodness' sake. It's not from the placenta, period. And calm down, stop screaming." "But what is it, then?" you scream. "I don't know, but it's just not the placenta. Put it in salty water, I'm on my way."

He arrives twenty minutes later. You've put the jelly in a storage jar, you're shaking from head to foot. He holds the jar up to eye level. "Just as I said, it's not placenta tissue. It's, they're…" he's choosing his words. "They're just ordinary villous tissues, it's…" "What did you say?" You hug your arms around your waist. "I'm not going to give you an anatomy lesson now, my poor child, it would be too complicated. But it's nothing, don't worry, it's completely normal. You'll just need a midwife to give your womb a little check tomorrow, that's all. So, a lot of fuss about nothing," he says, unscrewing the lid of the jar. And before you've had a chance to ask any more questions, he throws the contents into the toilet and flushes it. "There, all gone," he says.

"It was placenta tissue, no doubt about it," he tells Dr. Guerry senior that evening. "A good chunk. I don't know what happened but your son Charles totally lost it during my daughter's labor: he refused to give her a section when that's what was needed, and even afterward...How did he not check the delivery was complete? What a mistake! Even a beginner doesn't do that!" "I, yes, I don't understand. He must have been overwhelmed by the drama of it, he was thrown." "Luckily my daughter got up to go to her baby's funeral, because otherwise, if she'd stayed in bed, it would have stayed inside her, she could have had septicemia or worse...Can you imagine?" "I'm so sorry...Will she be, I mean, does she want to make an official complaint?" "No, all that's taken care of, there'll be no repercussions. My son-in-law wants an expert assessment of her case, but there'll be no mention in it of the placenta, you can be sure of that. Even the governing board won't know anything about it." "Thank you so much, my dear friend, your understanding does you credit. I don't know how to..." "It wouldn't bring the baby back, anyway. I'm doing this for your son, my friend, I know him: he's a brilliant boy, he'll settle in, he needs to be given a chance."

Your father hangs up. He feels relieved too, the weight of his remorse is eased with this oblation. If this went all the way up to the medical board, who knows what might come to light. He and your mother bumped into Charles Guerry two months ago when they were walking around the park outside city hall. The two men were happy to see each other again, and your mother thought Charles handsome, still such a good-looking boy; they traded news. Charles told them that he'd just set up his office as an obstetrician, and had very few patients at this stage but was hoping his books would fill up soon because he'd recently gotten divorced and had a lot of expenses. They wanted to help this promising boy, give him a leg up by entrusting their daughter to him. It was tricky, you were likely to resist, they had to find a way. That same evening, they talked it through at the living-room table, like in the fairy tale *Tom Thumb*; but unlike in the fairy tale, you weren't hiding behind the door, so you didn't hear them thinking of ways to lose you, you weren't there when they came up with the idea of telling you that your gynecologist was an alcoholic.

Two weeks later you and Christian are having dinner at your parents' house. Your mother has gone off to bed and the three of you are now in the living room drinking whiskey, with the TV on in the background. "I've been thinking," your husband says suddenly, glowering at the bottom of his glass as if it were an enemy, "I've been thinking about how to kill him." "Kill who?" You look at him, the almost black rings around his eyes, his clamped jaw. "Him. The fuckwit." You and your father glance at each other. "Without being caught, obviously," he adds, his eyes glazed, as if this detail should reassure you. "I won't go to prison for that bastard, oh no." He sits in silence for a moment; stoked by the alcohol, his grief is being mollified by hate and fantasies. "So, say I killed him at his office (I could just wait till his secretary's left), then I go straight to the airfield and fly to, maybe Hyères or Ajaccio, then I'd have an alibi." You're stunned. You're trying to think what to say when your father chips in, "No, no, that wouldn't give you an alibi, Christian" (he has reinstalled some formality since the funeral, calling Christian *vous* again). "Think it through: Everyone would know, I mean about the plane—the airfield here, the airfield at the other end, you'd have to let them know you were landing. The police would catch you straightaway." You're just feeling grateful to your father for adroitly shifting your husband's hallucinatory present tense to the conditional, when he starts talking again: "No, what it needs is for me to do it. My friend Georges from the Automobile Club, I'll borrow his Ferrari and hide it in the garage so no one sees me, then as soon as I've shot that total loser, I'll drive straight to Belgium or the Netherlands: doing two hundred kilometers an hour, no one would suspect that I was here when the crime was committed." "Yeah," says Christian, "but you'd be zapped by speed cameras on the way, there's no way you wouldn't be…" "Not if I plan my route in advance to avoid them." "Fine, but do you think you can keep up your speed if you don't take the highways? I'd be really surprised if you could manage more than one ten…" "With a Ferrari? Are you kidding?" "Yes, well, you need good reflexes and your eyesight's probably not that great, at your age." "I did the Monte Carlo rally as recently as last year, you know, Christian, I'm not that much of a has-been."

You watch them. Two little boys swaggering as they compare their pee-pees, their thingamabobs. They've already forgotten the reason for this conversation and are now plowing full steam ahead with their rockets and bathyscaphes, leaping astride their chargers, their steeds, their warhorses, ready to cross swords in the name of their sole ambition: being the best. Being better than whoever thinks he's best. They're quite touching (with their boys' grief), they're exasperating, they're abandoning you. You no longer have a husband or a father, you're a girl stranded in the real world, torn to shreds by a monster, and no king or king's son can save you from it.

A *few weeks after Tristan died,* you and Christian receive the expert's report. "Doctors have a commitment to tend, they do not have a commitment to specific results," the preamble reminds you. The report concludes that there was no medical error, but that it was "a case of bad luck": a cesarean would have given you a better chance of having a live baby is all that can be said. A case of bad luck... You weigh up the words, they weigh on you. A throw of the dice will never abolish chance. You didn't have all the luck on your side the day you gave birth, that's absolutely right, although you don't know to what extent it was lacking. Crucified on the altar of social connections, sacrificed to the medical profession with your feet up in stirrups, spread-eagled under a surgical light, this is the cruelest object-lesson scenario you've ever had to suffer, it isn't something you could have imagined. But this case of bad luck goes back a lot further, it's a very old story that some might wrongly assume was written for another place or in another age. The bad luck in this instance, here and now, lies in being someone who doesn't choose, who's manipulated, a pawn in a lie, the puppet in a plot, the stake in a tacit agreement, a person whose fate, whose life and heartbreak and joy are decided alongside her, outside her, in spite of her, by parents, masters, and men. The bad luck, you see, was being a girl.

Then one day you go to the hospital. You were told that you could come to pick up your son's medical file but never have. You eventually made an appointment and here you are. It's a foggy morning, Rouen looks as if it's emerging from the Middle Ages, you wouldn't be surprised to see the Maid of Orleans appear in all her armor. You don't know the doctor who sees you, he's a sort of mediator who can answer your questions should the need arise. You just ask him what a placenta looks like, he doesn't seem surprised and shows you an illustration—the blood vessels, the umbilical cord, the villous tissues. You don't say anything, you're remembering your father flushing the toilet. You chat about one thing and another. The doctor refers to your having had a "precious pregnancy" and you don't understand this expression, you know it can't possibly mean "expecting a boy," of course not, no one's that candid, but you really can't think what else it could mean, and the uncertainty quietly lacerates your womb— you yourself, you're quite sure of it, are not the fruit of a precious pregnancy. You also confide in him your concerns about the future. He's very kind, tells you that your medical files don't suggest that there's any obstacle to your having "another one." He smiles at you. You don't say anything, you're listening to those words. Because in French the "one" of "another one" is masculine, it's just a figure of speech, the masculine pulling rank on the feminine. But still. And as for "another." You don't want another, you want the same baby.

Then the doctor picks up an envelope. It contains photos of Tristan taken by the staff who were on duty (he calls Tristan by his name, you can't get over it), they're for you but you don't have to look at them now. You nod yes, you'd like to. He takes out the Polaroids and hands them toward you, you reach for them but the two of you—is it you? is it him?—aren't coordinated and the envelope falls to the floor. "Oh! We dropped it," he says. You lower yourself to pick it up, crouching as if next to his grave, to pull up weeds, and there he is. Tristan. Not in the photo. There, his body, in the room, and he loves you, and you love him. Neither a child nor a ghost, neither a real boy nor just a spirit. A presence but with no clear appearance, faceless and ageless, an apparition. But there, definitely there. And he loves you, and you love him. It's self-evident.

"I don't want another one. I want the same one. I want him."

Sitting in the car with the engine off, you remember reading an extract from Proust for the purposes of a translation exercise, a passage in which the narrator, who hasn't thought about his beloved late grandmother for a long time, crouches down to tie his bootlace and remembers that she used to make this gesture for him, long ago, when he was very tired. It's that movement—bending down toward his boot—that restores the memory of his grandmother and his overpowering love for her. When you bend down to pick up those photos, you yourself called to mind this passage from the book and with it this resurrection or rather "the terribly strange contradiction of what survives and what is annihilated," that particular absence. This experience will be back, don't worry—Tristan will be back, it's not over, that's a promise, you'll see him again, you will cause the reflex of his fleeting presence to recur, but only if you don't strive to make it happen, if you don't try to summon it. This moment of grace must be natural or, pfft, it evaporates... You're at home, in the street, or on a bus, alone or surrounded by people, you kneel to pick something up or refasten the strap on a shoe and there, without praying or thinking or anything, there's a pause, that feeling of an angel walking over your grave, and it's him, it's Tristan, that particular absentee—your boy on a little outing to live on in your heart.

three

"It's a girl."

Christian wasn't there for the five-month scan, I called him in China. I would have liked to keep my voice neutral, factual, but I failed. "Are you disappointed?" I asked. "Not at all," he said. "A girl's great too, I mean to say: a girl's equally great."

I went into the bedroom at the end of the corridor. All the clothes I'd bought or knitted for Tristan were put away in the bottom of the chest of drawers, I hadn't managed to decide whether I should throw them out. I knelt down (*hello there, my darling*) and took out the two little blue woolen bonnets, I'd made a pair of them back then, I don't know why, two pairs of socks and two baby vests, I'd made two of everything as if I'd been expecting twins. Before this latest scan I wondered whether a living baby could wear a dead one's clothes, or at least the clothes intended for a dead baby—was it dangerous, would I be passing on the grief or the bad luck, like the names that melancholy children sometimes inherited from a dead brother, like Van Gogh whose stillborn older brother was called Vincent—I remembered his feral blues, his yellows full of betrayed hopes, his end. Now that I knew I was expecting a girl (*it's not you I'm expecting, Tristan*), I doubted a girl could wear boys' clothes without running risks, wasn't it sacrilegious, a petty thriftiness that would have a pernicious effect on the child's development, obscene? Shouldn't I have immediately knitted new ones and thrown out these now that they were useless (*it's not you coming back, Tristan*)? In the end I kept everything, carefully folded in the chest of drawers. In the mirror I saw my gaunt face, my belly that was already huge, an oval ball. As a teenager, I'd occasionally seen my father's face in mirrors and this resemblance gave me concerns about my femininity as much as it reassured me about his paternity—I definitely was my father's daughter. For two years now it was Tristan that I'd been seeing: oh the baby in my features, his ivory-colored cheeks like an antique doll's—I definitely was my son's mother. *It's not you I'm expecting, Tristan. It's a girl.* I still talked to him but he was no longer alone. He knew that. I could feel him nestling into my memory, curling himself up small. I was sheltering a fetus and a ghost. I was half cradle, half coffin. *It's*...A hearty kick inside me brought the conversation to an end with a bang, like some-one slamming a drawer shut with their foot. I pulled a face, *your sister*. Then smiled and put my hand over my navel. She wasn't yet born but already had her own personality.

Sometimes, especially when Christian wasn't there, I would wake in the night bathed in sweat and I'd think I couldn't do this: daughters don't necessarily love their mothers, I told myself. Whereas of course a boy would love me. Would have loved me. Boys are all crazy about their mother, she's the love of their lives. But a girl? Or the question would be reversed: I myself had always adored my mother, but what about her? Did she love me? I had no idea. It was such a long time since my mother had said "I love you" to me. If I was to be the love of someone's life, whose would it be? I wondered. I felt useless, a girl but only just. I'd failed at everything.

In the last two years, but particularly since this new pregnancy, Christian had been away a lot, he'd moved up to be number two in his company. Our life together had become depressing. Every time we made love it hurt me. "It's perfectly normal," my father said when my mother reported the problem to him, "it's a normal effect of the episiotomy." Perhaps. But does it hurt less when it's nor-mal? So I'd restricted our—the word coitus came back to me with no warning; "Oh, great," Christian said, "why not call it copulation while you're at it?"—I'd restricted our (lovemaking, intercourse, intimacy) to the four days around my ovulation which I identified by taking my temperature. "So basically it's utilitarian fucking," Christian teased, and I resented his sarcasm which took no account of my pain and begrudged me for being *cold*. No one's acknowledging, no one has ever acknowledged that I might be in pain, I thought. Girls always complained about nothing. Even in my work I'd stopped looking for poems to translate, and saddled myself with scientific tomes, I didn't want to translate my suffering. I felt alone and kept my eye on the calendar. My old fears had been reversed: what I wanted more than anything was *to be late*. Two years had gone by in the hope of being late, of flouting regularity, and this in a life full of order and precision. Since the new pregnancy had been announced, everyone could breathe again. Christian didn't understand me. "For goodness' sake, have I given you a baby or not?" he would ask if he found me in tears. He was getting ahead of himself for a start, the baby could easily die. I no longer believed in immortality, I'd grown old. When a child died, eternity no longer existed. I was obsessed with a film that I'd once watched but now couldn't track down its name, one of those films where someone always asks for a basin of hot water before the birth, I've never understood why, anyway, in the film a doctor asks the dazed father if he wants "to keep the mother or the child," I thought about it all the time, the conjunction "or" weighed on the small of my back, I couldn't remember whom he chose but he was the one making the choice. As for my father, his diagnosis was very simple (first-year textbook): I was slightly depressed, very common in pregnancy, morning sickness, raging hormones, vitamins, magnesium, routine.

Alice was born in the Rouen hospital. Christian stayed out in the corridor, I didn't want him to be there. "I'd rather this was just between girls," I'd joked and he hadn't insisted. Shortly after the five-month scan we'd decided to call her Alice, so she can take us to wonderland, Christian had said; I personally preferred the idea of a rabbit making wishes over her cradle rather than men. She was big and beautiful, she weighed 3.8 kilograms. She hadn't suffered and neither had I, and lying in her cradle an hour after she was born, she was all pink. "Well, she'll never be a top model for pantyhose," said Christian, prodding her thighs as they wriggled in her sleepsuit. "Did you see her thighs? Like hams!" "She gets that from her mother," my father said, laughing. "Do you know what Laurence's nickname was when she was little? Luckily I kept a close eye on her or you'd have married a hot air balloon!"

When I started to open my nightshirt they left, their faces the picture of discretion, but they needn't have bothered: I didn't have any milk. The nurses took three days to realize this because Alice was often coupled to my breast, suckling furiously—and with good reason: she was getting nothing, or only a soothing sense of fusion which eventually sent her to sleep, apparently replete. But the weigh-ins were unambiguous: she was wasting away. We had to switch to bottles. "That's not good," my father kept saying tetchily, taking the midwife as a witness. "Colostrum and mother's milk are vital for a baby's health. Try harder," he added with every visit. "Try again." Try what? He even attempted to get Christian on his side. "Women these days are too worried about keeping their breasts a beautiful shape, it's outrageous," but my husband didn't answer, he stroked my arm, he must have thought it important that my breasts stayed a beautiful shape, even though we never made love anymore. Bottle-feeding Alice was torture for me: I was incompetent, not put together right to feed a baby. Did I subconsciously want to let her die? To watch her perish? Nourish, perish—I could feel madness lurking and then retreating in great inexplicable tides, death kicking gently at the cradle, just for fun. "If I have one piece of advice for you," my mother said a little later when Alice was whimpering, "it's don't pick her up when she cries at night, otherwise you'll exhaust yourself, especially because you're not breastfeeding so you'd have to get up to warm the bottle. Babies quickly learn they get everything by crying, you know, particularly girls."

And how do you know this then, Mom? I didn't say a thing.

For now, everyone's happy and relieved, except for me. I can't sleep at night, I'm frightened she'll die while I surrender my intentional vigil to sleep. The fear is killing me. Alice's life depends on my vigilance, and I'm so tired. I don't know how to be a mother, I can't do it. My mother knew how, she did it, even after Gaëlle. How did she manage that? I gulp down things that end in "-am" and "-ene," as she does. I consult a specialist in baby blues. I read books about childbirth in which love is spontaneous, I compare myself—and condemn myself. What will happen to us? I wonder privately.

Then one night the exhausted sentry that I've become hears Alice crying. It's not great howls of pain or hunger, rather a lonely mewling, or am I the one who's so alone, lying wrapped in my insomnia next to my sleeping husband? In the early weeks Christian got up more often than I did, but now he sleeps; the handover happened tacitly, he passed the buck—the baby—to me. When she cries at night, I go to her, I ignore my mother's advice; I always go to her when she cries, and never without a feeling of terror. No sleeping pill gets me over that frontier which would distance me from everything that's going on, every rustling sound and threat. Life dies, that's all I know. On this particular night, I listen for only a few seconds before getting up. I go over to her cot where she's wriggling and whimpering in the bluish glow of her rabbit night-light. Hovering on the edge of the shadows, I say, "I'm here," I'm talking to myself more than to her, reassuring myself in my sleepwalking existence. When I step into the pool of light, she stops immediately. I can see her breathing beneath the rabbit on her sleepsuit. I lean over her as characters lean over lakes in fairy tales, a shiver runs through her, "momomo," she says, "yes," I say, "I'm here," she murmurs, "momomo," she mumbles, waving her hands, "momommy." Oh! I lean a little closer, "momommy." It's the first time. She's been saying "more" for a month now, more fruit puree, more cuddles, but "mommy" is a new word, newborn, and the thing itself is born along with the word. Momommy. It's so sudden and clear-cut, such an eloquent whispering: I am her mother. The event takes shape and takes root, intertwining branches reach out. Such fertile soil! Alice's eyes latch onto mine, they're luminous, tender, mischievous, so many emotions in such young eyes that have still seen so few things, it truly is unbelievable. I say yes, I'm here (love is being there), and she says "momommy" again, "mygirl," I say, mirroring her, "momommy," she repeats the word, "mygirl," I say again, "momommy," she gurgles, and she laughs, I mean really laughs, and we both laugh in the bluish darkness.

Alice is eighteen months old. Yesterday evening she pointed to the sky and said "moon," and this morning she pressed her nose to a window battered by the privet hedge and said "wind." She says these words with no article, in a fairylike voice so imperious that things seem to be born as they emerge from her mouth, summoned. I woke her early this morning, as I do every day, to take her to her nanny Joëlle who has two sons aged three and four and is expecting a third. Just as I try to put on the knitted green sleeve of her dress, she shakes her arm free, it's not the first time she's done this, and she runs off to the other end of the room in her pull-up diaper. "No dess," she enunciates exaggeratedly, "no dess," she stamps her feet and climbs onto her rocking horse. I walk toward her with the dress, we don't have time for this, she takes it and throws it against the wall like a handful of sand, "no dess," she says, her voice firm, she's looking at me and laughing but this isn't for fun, she's waiting for her will to be done, "no dess." "Damn it, Alice," I leave the dress scrunched up on the floor, "we're going to be late," I put her in a sweater and overalls, and she sings.

It's her birthday, she's three. She's asked her grand-mother for a cowboy costume after watching a Western on TV with her father. The Stetson is a little too big for her, she flips it back dismissively, snapping the heels of her boots together and making the spurs rattle. I meanwhile am her wife, I bake cakes in the hearth to feed the twelve teddy bears we have together. "Good morning, wife," she says, bursting into the kitchen wearing a serious expression, "I can't stay long, I have things to do." "You should have come and helped me knead the dough," I say, but she's already left. Her rocking horse is waiting for her, tethered to the floor lamp in the living room. She takes big strides like her father who is busy mending a wall sconce, and gives a stamp of her foot, bringing one hand up to her temple. "Captain," she says, "we have a problem. The Indians are here." Screwdriver in hand, Christian salutes her earnestly. "General," he replies with considerable emotion in his voice, "we have another problem…" "We do?" asks Alice, jutting her chin and knitting her brows. "Yes, General, a serious problem: I love you." Alice gives him a slap, "Stop it, Daddy," then they both fall about laughing.

I'm in square des Alouettes, it's winter and there are still traces of snow along the gravel paths. Alice is wearing a blue anorak and she's pulled the hood up over her knit cap. "She looks like a garden gnome," her father said earlier before setting off to the airfield. Alice soon abandons the slide in favor of the monkey bars, swinging on one and watching the boys before copying what they're doing. The admiration in her eyes as she watches them is so intense that I look away—but she doesn't even see me, anyway: boys pretend to forget that they have a mother. Hup, she hangs upside down from a bar and easily swings from one to the next. "Your son's very good at that," says a mother sitting next to me on the bench. "Very sure of his own abilities. Mine's much clumsier." I smile weakly (I should have let her braid hang down out of her cap). "It's a girl," forms behind my lips, crashes against my teeth and melts under my tongue. "Thank you," I say.

Alice is four and she's going to the tennis courts with her father for her first lesson with the mini club. Christian plays on the next court while the instructor gets to know her group of children, asking them all their names. There's Jasmine, Léa, Jules, Alexis, and Jordan. "What about you?" "My name's Oddjob," Alice tells her. "Oddjob? Are you sure? That's not a name..." Alice is perfectly calm: "Yes, that's me. My name's Oddjob." She starts to look for her father so the instructor doesn't persist. There sure are some wacky parents! There was a little boy called Rolex at Club Med once, and another year there was a girl called Peanut. But really... Oddjob, for a girl... and plus it's Oddjob Charpentier—Oddjob Carpenter... Well, it's a free world. "Oddjob has quite an aptitude," she tells Christian at the end of the session. He stands there open-mouthed, Alice eyes him sideways, he looks as if he's swallowed his tennis racket and a power drill into the bargain. His account of the episode chills me: there's something wrong with our daughter. I feel a whole world of foreboding resurfacing from underground. Christian shrugs, says, "No, no, she already has really good coordination, you should have seen her with her mini racket!" I don't understand until two months later when she and I go back to the home improvement store Mr. Oddjob to buy some door handles; we'd been going there for weeks while we were fixing up our new house. I'm Mrs. Charpentier, that's what the sales staff call me. But she, Alice, wanted to have a man's name.

"*What brings you here?*" asks the pediatrician, folding his hands under his chin.

I've been talking to him for twenty minutes. I've told him about Tristan, Alice's birth, Mr. Oddjob...Hasn't he listened to any of it? Still, I answer politely.

"As we explained on the phone, we're worried."

He smiles fleetingly, but not with his eyes, they stay steely. He's not bad-looking, and would definitely be better without the beard. Why did I say "we" when I'm all on my own? I *am* all on my own, that's the truth of it. Increasingly alone.

"Our four-year-old daughter, Alice, says she's a boy."

"Yes."

"She wants to be a boy. We don't know what to do."

"How do you mean what to do?"

I look away. "Well..."

"Does she say she's a boy," he asks, "or is it you saying that she wants to be a boy?"

"I...it..." I stammer.

"Or perhaps it's that you want her to be a boy?"

And now I'm already in the dock, it's always the same with shrinks, mothers have to plead their case—mothers alone. I falter and then pull myself together.

"The thing is, it's...Alice has always wanted this. She...she never wants to wear dresses or skirts, I'd love her to, I buy them for her, you know...The other day her nanny wanted to paint her nails, it has to be said she has three boys so she likes playing with a little girl, but Alice threw a terrible tantrum and knocked over the nail polish. She practices peeing standing up in the bath, she abandons all the dolls she's given, tossing them in a corner, and only likes plushies. At school she only plays with the boys, well, she tries to, they don't really let her play soccer with them, which makes her angry."

"I see."

I smile.

"I understand why she's angry. I don't see..."

"She talks about herself as male, she says, 'Alice, he's handsome' and 'Alice, he's strong,' she thinks—"

"Children don't really grasp grammar until they're four or five, or gender identity for that matter, they don't use appropriate pronouns, it's absolutely normal."

"Some coworkers of my husband's came for lunch last Sunday. One man bent down to kiss Alice hello and said, 'Don't you look pretty in your Mickey Mouse T-shirt!' Well, she stood squarely in front of him, offered her hand to shake, and said 'I's handsome.'"

"Just as I was saying... grammar's no—"

I keep adding to my examples, I feel like an informant.

"And when he retorted gently, 'No, you're not, you're pretty, you're a girl,' she stamped her foot and shook her head. She wouldn't back down so he explained: 'You were born a girl so you're a girl, a pretty little girl. And I was born a boy so I'm a boy,' and she got angry, saying, 'Me too. I was a boy.'"

"She's right."

"Excuse me?"

"Yes, your daughter's right in a way: your baby was a boy."

I'm speechless.

"I imagine you told her about her big brother? She knows he died?"

The expression "big brother" paralyzes me: Alice is four years old and Tristan's so tiny...

"Yes, I've told her about him right from when she was born."

"Why?"

"It was another psychologist, a woman, who advised me to." He can hear the note of triumph in my voice, how glad I am that I can justify myself, that I have this endorsement. I'm authorized. "I suffered a sort of depression after she was born, I was scared of everything, scared she'd die like her brother, scared she'd fall, scared I was doing it wrong. I had so much anxiety that the psychologist at the hospital told me I should try explaining why to Alice. Babies understand everything, you can talk to them, right? Well, that's what I did, I picked her up one day and started talking to her very quietly. I told her that if I seemed anxious and awkward, it was because I'd lost a little boy before she was born, it had made her daddy and me very sad, but . . ."

He clenches his jaw, vents his irritation on a pencil that he drives into a chamfered eraser which already has more holes in it than a colander.

". . . but I loved her and I was so happy she was there. Your colleague adv—"

"She's not my colleague. I'm a psychiatrist, not a psychologist. How old was Alice?"

"Oh, she'd just been born, she was maybe two weeks old, or three . . ."

He sighs.

"Do you think it was a mistake, Doctor? She didn't understand?"

He sniffs. "Quite the opposite, Alice understood perfectly, she's most likely a very intelligent little girl. She understood that you were sad because you lost a little boy."

"You mean . . ." I can't get my brain to think. I've read that you can drive someone mad by giving them contradictory instructions. Should I have talked to Alice or shouldn't I? What does science have to say about it? What's the truth? Is it my fault if . . . "You mean it's my fault? Alice thought we wished she was Tristan, is that it? Is that why she's a tomboy?"

He puts down his eraser and pencil, and smiles at me. It's not a well-meaning smile.

"A tomboy? What do you mean exactly?"

I hate him. Do I really have to define every term, even the most everyday expressions? He's growing his beard to look like Freud, I'm sure of it.

"Have you noticed," he continues in a slightly superior tone, "there's no opposite equivalent of tomboy, no tomgirl? That's because no boy—or hardly any—longs to be a girl, whereas...a tomboy is a girl who's been denied the freedom to be a boy. Not being free, that's what girls suffer. Don't you feel it yourself?"

His eyes bore into me. My cheeks flush, I squirm in my chair, crossing and uncrossing my legs.

"But do we have a choice? Is it—"

"In Alice's case," he interrupts me, "I think it's more complicated. She doesn't just want to be *a* boy, she wants to be a specific boy. A particular boy. You want to call her a tomboy? No. Let's say more a missing boy, a lost boy."

Tears swell in the corners of my eyes, please don't let them fall, I'm wearing mascara. I must stay presentable.

"Alice wants to give you Tristan back, that's all. It's as simple as that."

"But why?"

He raises his eyebrow, stands up, and sees me to the door. "Wednesday at four o'clock, with Alice," he says.

Alice doesn't want to see the child psychiatrist but she does it to please me. She looks at me with kind, questioning eyes, this consultation will probably benefit me. I yelled at her yesterday for tearing the ribbon off her slippers, she thought it was "ugly." I sewed it back on overnight, so she spent the whole morning trailing around the house in her socks. She extends her left hand to the doctor with a brusque spontaneity, and he shakes it with his right hand.

"Are you left-handed?" he asks her. "Me too. But we're still supposed to shake with our right hands, you and me. It's what people call a convention, something people do to keep everybody happy, not make any trouble. It's convenient, you see. But don't worry, we're still left-handed, we don't give up on what we are. Go ahead, have a go."

Alice laughs, she thrusts out her right hand several times as if producing a pistol, and he laughs along with her. The three of us go into his office.

"Do you know why you're here?" the doctor asks. Alice shakes her head.

"Your mommy's worried, she says you want to be a boy. Is that right?"

"Yes."

"Why?"

Alice looks at me.

"No, don't ask Mommy. Give me your answer. Why do you want to be a boy?"

She raises her chin, shrugs her shoulders right up to her ears and lets them fall back down with a sigh. "Because...I want to live like a boy," she says.

"Of course, Alice!" the doctor says approvingly. "You're right: you want to live. Just look, you're alive!"

Alice laughs out loud, jumps up from her chair, and runs around the room with her arms out like an airplane.

"I alive," she sings, "I alive," then she wraps her arms around her knees and hugs them in tight.

Once we're back home and I'm having a drink in the living room with Christian, who's perplexed by my description of the appointment—"all that dumbass messing around with words"—Alice appears with her father's razor, scraping it over her cheek as she's seen him do so often. I stifle a scream, Christian left it lying around by the basin, he doesn't think, never foresees anything, I have to think of everything, all the time, avoiding things that could hurt Alice, anticipating and preempting others that could kill her, planning and providing those that will improve her well-being, her happiness, our lives. I've had enough, I'm tired. "So what am I supposed to say!" Christian rejoins, opening one of his files.

I take Alice to see Dr. B. every two weeks. I now stay in the waiting room where I can hear their peals of laughter. She sometimes makes drawings. One time he asks her to do a drawing of herself with her mommy and daddy, but as animals. When she proudly hands me the piece of paper at the end of the session, I see a very elongated oval shape with black dashes all around the outside. "It's a millipede," she explains. "Good call," I say with a forced laugh, "mommies never stop running." She's drawn her father as an elephant, with a disproportionately long trunk dragging on the ground—he'd be happy if only he were here—and herself as an elephant calf of more modest proportions, but still, the tiniest flick of its trunk would pulverize a whole nest of millipedes. All around us on the savanna trees with penis-shaped tops stand proudly alongside phallic mushrooms with red caps. Dr. B. smiles broadly. The millipede now looks like exactly what it is, a vulva, a drab vulva surrounded by dense hairs. I feel stupid, standing there clutching my portrait.

Alice's little school is very close to the house we've bought in Canteleu, in the countryside around Rouen. When I'm not immersed in a tricky translation, I hear the bell for recess and hurry up to the second floor to watch—I hide behind her bedroom curtain, I don't want her to see me, she'll think I'm keeping tabs on her. She's always with boys. At the start of the year she stood to one side and studied them, she took in the rules of the game, then one day she ventured out and took up a position at random on one of the teams. They couldn't believe it at first, the new girl wanted to play soccer! What the hell! The girls with their skipping ropes were transfixed too, and my heart pounded from behind that window. I both dreaded and longed for her to be rejected. She's now their best goalkeeper—I watch her modestly saving goals with her mittens, which she never fails to take with her, even in summer. "Alice, Alice, come to my house!" shout the boys on the teams. "I'll give you some candy." Sometimes she doesn't play, but stays on the sidelines talking to Kevin, their hair almost touching. He's the son of the Durands who run the garage at the end of our street, a lovely-looking boy with brown hair and very dark eyes. The two of them go into the colorful log cabin that has pride of place in the middle of the youngest children's schoolyard, and they stay there for all of recess, I don't see them at all. "What's inside that log cabin, sweetheart? Games?" "No, there's nothing, it's just a cabin." "So what do you do in there?" "We do loving," Alice replies. Her childish terminology affords me a sense of relief but I can't shake off the fear buried within it.

Kevin gives Alice dainty bracelets, necklaces of pink beads, and floral scrunchies for her ponytail. His mother smiles at me conspiratorially by the school gates, cute little lovebirds. Alice accepts these gifts with an embarrassed smile, she brings them home and then gives them to me: jewelry's for girls, it's not great for playing soccer, it bounces around and goes bling bling. However much I insist, she never wears any of it, even to please Kevin.

In early May the school starts working on its end-of-year show. An information sheet is sent out to parents. "Note for moms—last-year nursery-school children: Charleston flapper-style dress, headband, and string of beads for girls; black suit, retro vest, and white shirt for boys. NB: Mrs. Sanchez is available for sewing work. Contact her at 5 place de l'Église." Two sketches in black felt-tip drawn by the teacher indicate the Roaring Twenties mood of the planned choreography. "I'm going to take this piece of paper and show it to Mrs. Sanchez," I tell Alice the following Wednesday. "Are you coming?" Alice doesn't move from the branch in the medlar tree that she's straddling like a gaucho out on the pampa. "Come on, Alice, let's get going, I'm worried there'll be lots of people." (I'll be the only person there, I'm sure of it: all the mommies here can sew.) "There's no point," she says. Marco, her most faithful teddy bear who's riding behind her, seems to agree, his small dark eyes stare at me glumly. "You need to be there so you can be measured." Alice kicks her spurs into the medlar's trunk and leans forward as the tree sets off at a gallop, Marco clings to her and her words reach me through the wind-rustled leaves, "No, there's no point making a dress." I close the gate onto the street with a sigh. "Alice. I know you don't like wearing dresses. But this time you have to: it's the costume for the show." She curls her lip the way she does when I serve her beetroot. "Well, I don't want to." "All the girls have to be dressed the same, do you understand? It's a dance. You must have started rehearsing, haven't you?" She says, "Yes, but without the dress." I smile. "It's just for the day of the show, my darling." She doesn't respond. "Okay, here's what I suggest: we'll go get it made, then you can see," I say, full of hypocrisy (it's a foregone conclusion). "I won't wear it," she says, full of sincerity (that's a foregone conclusion too).

"I understand," the psychiatrist says on the phone. Alice stopped seeing him more than six months ago— "This child is absolutely fine"—but Christian's in Japan for three months and I don't know who to confide in with my guilty anxieties. "Explain that this is theater, put it to her as a game, as dressing up, which she likes, role-play." "But I've already said all that!" I reply irritably, the guy claims to understand but he doesn't understand anything. "Or give her the collective spirit angle: she's contributing to the success of the show, it's like a soccer team, everyone wears the same strip." Good metaphor, thank you, Doctor, I already thought of that. "Well then, why don't we all wear soccer shirts?" Alice retorted. Doesn't he have more illuminated ideas, then, any clearer instructions? This is no longer just semantics. Hasn't Alice always had a problem with identity? "It doesn't work like that," he says. "An item of clothing doesn't determine femininity. The dress doesn't make the girl, you know." I'm standing next to the landline phone, in the mirror I can hardly make out my own body in the shapeless tracksuit I've been wearing nonstop since Christian went away—I put it on the moment I get up or as soon as I'm home. "Yes, okay. But then what am I supposed to do?" Who's going to deal with my distress, lift away the slab of marble weighing on my chest, drive back my terror that I don't fit the mold, that I'm not capable (of sewing, being a woman, being loved)? Can someone look after me, take me in their arms, care about me with all their heart? "Try again," he says. I'm about to hang up, defeated, when he adds: "Otherwise..." "Yes?" "Otherwise give up."

The girls come on from stage right and the boys stage left, and a jazzy Charleston trumpet tune bursts exuberantly to life. The teacher is hiding behind the curtains; from where I'm sitting I can see her contorting herself ahead of the beat, feeding the steps to the most bewildered, the ones scanning the room for their mothers. The two rows of children face each other, they draw together and then part, almost touching, then pushing away again; they wave their arms, thrust their feet forward, their hands crisscross wildly over their knees. The boys pretend to smoke, smooth down their slicked hair, and hold the lapels of their jackets; the girls have swirly fringed dresses, lipstick, and here and there a plumed headdress; some of them have shoes with heels (made to fit five-year-olds), they simper, making their beads swing and bounce. I'm dressed as a butterfly—is a butterfly a boy or a girl thing?—in the schoolyard in Rouen, I'm five years old too, my antennae have just got caught up in Jeannine's and everyone's laughing at us, I'm sweating, I wipe my forehead, dripping with shame. "Did you forget to put her dress on?" whispers the woman next to me, half catty, half purring indulgence.

My heart thuds, I want to cry. "No," I say matter-of-factly, "she didn't want to wear it." These words are immediately transmitted all around the hall, where most eyes are already turned on me—the reply of the century, oh my, we won't forget this in a hurry: *She didn't want to.* A little kid knee-high to a grasshopper! Great job on parental authority! Just imagine the mess in their house! The father's never there, that's why.

The jazz trumpet suddenly starts its cancan but I've stopped hearing, I've stopped seeing. My eyes are pinned on Alice who's performing her part to the letter, staying on her mark, keeping time, throwing out her arms in perfect rhythm, smiling when they change sides, twirling her Charleston around the stage so lightly, gracefully, easily, and naturally it's a knockout. The shame vanishes, I'm overwhelmed with admiration. Opposite her, the dark brooding Kevin, who looks panicked under his brilliantine, can't decide whether it's absurd or wonderful to be dancing with a partner in checkered dungarees and Velcroed sneakers. He feels the same as me: stunned. Standing at the foot of the stage, his father, Régis Durand, of Durand Garage, is stony-faced, offended; he turns off his video camera.

A few months later it's December and Santa comes to give presents to the nursery-school children. The girls are given a little cart of housekeeping utensils (a broom, bucket, floor mop, and dustpan and brush—all in pink), the boys a LEGO set. "No one's ever complained before," the astonished principal assures me when I relay Alice's displeasure and ask awkwardly for an explanation. "In fact little girls just love imitating their mommies." "It can't do any harm," Christian says before flying off to Tokyo. "But why pink? It's such a cliché." That evening Alice and I take a bath together. She's wearing the bucket as a hat with the handle under her chin, and is flicking water at me with the hand brush. "You'll just have to ask Kevin if you can play with his LEGO set with him," I tell her. Alice gives a casual pout. "I don't really talk to Kevin these days." "Really? Isn't he your boyfriend anymore?" "No." "Why?" "He likes Charlotte better now. He thinks she dresses better... Pfff," she adds, smacking the bucket with the dustpan. I laugh and she laughs with me. I'm dazzled by her healthy young body in the bubbles.

One summer Sunday I'm watching Alice and Christian from the second-floor window that looks out over the yard, they're by the swimming pool. Christian started teaching her to swim a few days ago, but she's still scared of going into the water without a rubber ring. He asks her to climb down into the water with him, she doesn't want to, no part of the pool is in her depth. Her father insists, tells her she's a scaredy-cat, tries to grab her; she ducks aside and runs around the pool screaming, but he catches her, "No, no, I don't want to!" he picks her up, I watch her legs scramble frantically against her father's chest, "No!"

she howls, the panties of her bikini have slipped halfway down her backside, "No, Daddy, let me go," "Oh, she's such a scaredy-cat," he says again and throws her in the water.

I race downstairs—he threw her like a garbage bag, like pig swill, like a corpse. "But, look, I came in to get her straightaway," he says when I yell, "Not her, no, not her!" He climbs out of the water and sets Alice down on the grass, she's silent, her eyes full of tears. "I dived in and got her. She's just annoyed, that's all, she's gone into a sulk, right, sweetheart, you're sulking? Were you scared? Really? But nothing bad can happen to you when Daddy's here."

"What did you mean earlier when you said 'Not her'? How do you mean not her? Are you going to answer me? Are you sulking too? Like mother, like daughter. What the hell is wrong with you today? Is it your time of the month or something?"

We can't always see the end of love. But sometimes we do. Sometimes we can even put a date on it.

I look at myself in the bathroom mirror, with wet hair and no makeup, I look more and more like my father. What am I doing here? What are we doing here? Christian's only ever in transit and we're suffocating. "Would you like to live in Paris?" I ask Alice splashing the water. "No, where's Paris?"

I've applied for an interpreting job with UNESCO and eventually secure it. The soccer team at Canteleu nursery school's lost its best goalie but their loss is the gain of a small primary school in the fourteenth arrondissement of Paris—there's a whole new law governing these player transfers now: the Mercato law. "Why do you never play with the girls?" I ask Alice. (Did I think the capital would change her preferences?) "That's not true," she replies. "I do, sometimes. But the girls are annoying, they're always saying 'Well then you're not my friend anymore!' and I never even know why. At least boys stay friends, they don't argue."

That's not always the case. My divorce from Christian comes through the following summer. "Love's boat has broken up on the rocks of everyday life," says the Maya-kovsky epigraph in the novel I've just finished translating.

My parents also get a divorce. Since retiring, my father's been spending a lot of time at the Automobile Club and he bumped into a former patient there, Elsa, and what with the walks and the conferences they grew close. She's single and has always been in love with him, ever since she came to see him about her anorexia when she was sixteen—that was in 1978, he's dug out the medical record. He managed to wrest her from its clutches, you could say she owes him her life. She's still very slim, very pretty, and... "I can see you're trying to do the math," says my father. "Well, there's a twenty-nine-year age gap, that's a lot, I know, but love couldn't care less about the years so we've gotten close, we went on lots of little trips with the group, we... well, anyway, she's pregnant." "What about Mom?" "Your mother? No, she's not pregnant, oh wait, forgive me, that was bad taste. Well, your mother, your mother nothing, I told her I'd met someone, she's coming to terms with it, what do you expect, she doesn't have a choice."

Met someone, I think to myself. He should be saying he's met someone *else*. Or has my mother never actually been anyone?

My mother doesn't seem too rattled, though, even if her rival's age makes her sick—the woman's three years younger than I am. "Anyway, your father snores so much I haven't slept properly for years, so I'm happy to hand over the baton. It's not exactly a gift! Do you know what Sacha Guitry said when his wife Yvonne Printemps asked for a divorce so she could marry her friend Pierre Fresnay: 'I'm

going to have the cruelest revenge: I'll let him have her.'"
She only lost it briefly when I told her Elsa was expecting a
baby. The pain flitted across her face like a memory. "How
absurd! At his age! He'll look like a great-grandfather at
the school gates, if he gets that far!" She said nothing for a
minute, then asked, "Do you know if it's a girl or a boy?"
I shook my head. "They probably don't know yet," I said,
"she's only five months..." My mother then batted the
subject away with a flick of her hand, got up to fetch her
blood-pressure pill and swallowed it, staring blankly at the
wall in front of her. "It doesn't matter either way," she
said. "If it's a girl, they'll try again."

Life in Paris is tougher and more expensive but not lone-
lier. Christian has moved to Tokyo and Alice visits him as
soon as she has a vacation; she gives me a kiss at the airport then trots off with the stewardess without a backward
glance, she goes through customs with her teddy bear in
her arms and her soccer ball in her backpack—she'll play
with her father. I stay behind the barrier, watching her
determined stride and her blond braid swinging over
her panda bag. The first day after she leaves I no longer
exist, I have no reason left to be here, I sleep with my nose
buried in her pillow. Then I come through the air lock,
the mother in me withdraws, and I spend my evenings
on the Meetic dating site. I try to guess whether the men

I'm messaging have nice shoulders, I wish I could relive that first time at the Saint-Saëns swimming pool, when my desire wasn't as listless as a child who no longer wants to play. But I don't dare ask for a photo of their chests or their backs, even though they don't hesitate to ask to see my breasts. Sometimes I find a man who understands that being on all fours in bed doesn't mean you've landed on your feet in life. But it's a rarity. I translate more and more poetry, "never give all the heart," the line resonates for me. I'm also translating something for UNESCO, a report by a professor of gender studies (I didn't know what that was) who specializes in the connections between feminism and religion. I'm terrified by the welter of questions she raises, questions that fall back down heavily on my own life, even though it's a long time since I've been a Protestant. She quotes some words from Hélène Cixous about the massacre of firstborn children in Egypt, described in Exodus: "If it's a boy, kill him; if it's a girl, let her live (in other words, kill her in other ways)."

I take the train to Rouen and take a taxi to the clinic in Redon where Elsa had her baby yesterday. She's alone in her room, pale and euphoric, with the baby sleeping in a tiny crib beside her. A bottle of champagne stands open on the nightstand, alongside two Duralex glasses. I come closer. "Don't wake him," Elsa whispers, "he just had a feed. You'll get a better look at him later. Matthieu says he looks like you, he's the spitting image of you when you were born, but as a boy." He's dressed all in white with a small band of blue plastic on one wrist: Adam. So I have a brother who's 50 centimeters long and weighs 3.5 kilograms. So I have a brother who's ten years younger than my daughter. "You didn't call him Jean-Matthieu," I say. She opens her eyes wide and laughs. "Jean-Matthieu? Don't, that's so hillbilly. I'd rather die!" "That's what Dad wanted my name to be if I was a boy." "Yes, Matthieu told me that! Thank goodness you're a girl!" "Yes," I say, "thank goodness." She laughs again, silently. "You had a narrow escape . . . Do you like Adam, as a name?" "Yes, it's a good name. A bit heavy laden with the weight of the world: the first man, that's quite something. But a good name." In the ensuing silence some birds fly across the sky. It's a gray day. I wonder what it would have been like to have had a brother before. I don't know. My current brother could be my child. My son, I think to myself. "Yes," Elsa picks up the conversation, "you're right, Adam's quite a dense sort of name. But you're father's so happy it's a boy. So happy. You can't imagine."

A few birds alight on chimneys, some of which are smoking already. The fall is here.

A woman in a white coat comes into the room. It's Dr. Dubecq. Elsa introduces me: "My daughter-in-law." I think we've met, her eyes say. "I . . . I'll go, I'll leave you alone. Elsa, I'm...I'll be in the corridor." I sit in the waiting room surrounded by the building blocks that have been left out to mollify brothers and sisters. People come past with flowers, babies cry. A text from Christian lets me know that Alice has arrived safely in Tokyo. I retie the laces on my sneakers, or am I falling to my knees? Tristan's little knit cap peeps around the door, he's spotted the building blocks. *No, my darling, not now, please.* I close my eyes to kiss him anyway, then he disappears. Dr. Dubecq...how can it be?

"But of course your father knows," Elsa exclaims a little later. "She's my gynecologist! She delivered me! Matthieu was there! What? Alcoholic? What the hell are you talking about? Dr. Dubecq's never been alcoholic. I've been with her for years, she's wonderful, very professional. Where did you come up with a story like that? That's total slander. Dr. Guerry? No, I don't know him. Are you leaving already? Won't you wait till Adam wakes up? Your father should be here any minute. What's the matter?"

I run away, leaving by the emergency stairs, and every step confirms the evidence: my father hasn't told Elsa my story. Not worth it. No point. Whatever happens I mustn't see him, no coming back, no questions, no explanations, no amazement, no pain. Stop all this attention-seeking.

My train's not due for another forty-five minutes. I could call my mother, we could go to the cemetery at Toussaint, we could visit Gaëlle and Tristan. But I'd rather find a cybercafe and see what Meetic has to offer in Rouen, if there's an Ali Baba's cave, an Aladdin's lamp, something.

In the train on the way home there's a man walking along the corridor. "Daniel?" I say. He retraces his steps. "Laurence…" His cheeks flush pink, his emotion is so obvious that it touches me. "May I?" He sits next to me. "Wow, it's been a long time…" He still lives in Paris where he's a juvenile court judge, but he often makes the return trip to Rouen to see his elderly parents. After two divorces he now lives with a psychologist whom he recently met in court. He has no children of his own, but has plenty inside his head, his work consumes him body and soul, a real passion. He's happy to talk, going into details, and seems pleased by this chance meeting. He has no hair left but there's still a sort of gentleness in his eyes. I listen to him, that's something I'm good at. "How about you?" he says eventually. "What wonderful things have you been up to in all these years?" "Me? Nothing very interesting. Well, actually yes I have: I've had two children," I hear myself say for the first time. "A boy and a girl." "Oh! That's great—a pigeon pair! What are their names? Do you have photos?" "Wait, tell me about your story" (*I'm evasive, forcing my voice to sound light*), "that's intriguing: meeting someone in court? It must be unusual, right? Like something in a book, anyway." "Not at all, it's actually very common. Judges always take advice from psychologists, particularly when children are involved. They're invaluable when it comes to deciding whether children are telling the truth or being manipulated by one of their parents. And for spotting trauma, mistreatment, abuse, and rape." "And is there a lot of that?" "Very much so. You can't imagine. I remember you put the words 'Family, I hate you' up in your bedroom. I was kind of shocked at the time, but when it comes down to it, you were right."

I hesitate for a moment, I feel like talking too. In a detached voice I tell him that, when I was little, I too was... I can't find the word but I tell him about it. "I didn't know," he says, disconcerted and vaguely ashamed, as if he hadn't fulfilled his mission as an upholder of the law. It's a trait I find touching in men like him, the way they feel guilty for failing to protect a woman. "You couldn't know," I say. "And it doesn't matter at all. I'm fine, as you can see!" He eyes me silently, as if trying to gauge whether that's true.

"Let's see each other again," he says in the crowds at the end of the platform, and he hands me his business card. "You'll call me, won't you? Is that a promise?" I nod. We kiss goodbye. And he disappears into the station concourse. But he hasn't disappeared from my life now, has he, I think. Once I get home, though, I can search all I like, I've lost his card.

On *weekends*, Alice's school friends come for sleepovers. At first there were girls, but Alice doesn't like playing fashion shows or putting sequins in her hair or pouring scorn on boys but doing nothing but talk about them, she explains, so the girls didn't come back. When the fourth grade goes to the swimming pool, she doesn't wear her bikini top even though I put it in her bag. It's shameful, the girls think; the boys think it strange, super daring, a girl with nothing on top. The teacher defuses the situation and calls me that same evening: the solution for next time will be for Alice to wear a one-piece suit. "Yes, yes, of course," I say, and my fears are back, stampeding in my chest. Meanwhile, Alice can't see the problem at all. "Look, Momsy," she says, thrusting out her chest, "I'm like the boys, I have exactly the same little circles as them." She's right but I'd rather she didn't know that, I'd rather she followed the rules. Either way, thanks to Christian, she's a very good swimmer, she takes out everyone in the front crawl race, even the big kids in fifth grade, she tells me proudly. So the girls have withdrawn but it's not long before the boys show up: those who want to play on Game Boys that they're forbidden at home, those who love soccer, those who are in love with Alice—often all three categories at the same time. When she's on her own she builds Kapla fortresses and hurls Playmobil warriors at the walls, yelling, "Attack!" From my bedroom where I'm working, I hear her telling stories of boats and soldiers, she plays all the characters, adopting different voices with varying degrees of gruffness. "Launch the attack," she says. "Yes, sir!" she replies. When she tires of this performance, she calls me to come and play marbles. I don't make her beg but come running, indulging an age-old thwarted longing when I used to watch the boys playing this game in their schoolyard. She has a wonderful collection, and we roll and ricochet them around the apartment between the feet of various pieces of furniture—steelies, comets, taws, and aggies. "You see that one," she says, "it's a swirl, I won it yesterday, Paul Beuchet wasn't happy, and said 'Anyway, swirls are for girls,' I don't see why, and anyway, swirl, girl, it's practically the same. Who cares, Paul's a softie. Oh, look at that one, the dragon. It's beautiful!" There's also a firecracker, a cricket, a dragonfly, and a spiderman. She sifts them like jewels in her achingly pretty hands then suddenly slews them in every direction. In the evenings I read *Harry Potter* to her. Or I tell her the story of *Alice in Wonderland*, which she agrees to because of the name, and also because that particular Alice is afraid of nothing and doesn't think twice before following the White Rabbit. At the library she chooses Lucky Luke albums. One day my mother brought her the Bécassine books I'd had as a child in Rouen. Alice glanced at the title—*Do I want to read a book about a girl whose name means she's dumb?* I could see her thinking—she politely flicked through a few pages, peered closely at an illustration, and exclaimed, "Granny, Mommy, look...Bécassine doesn't have a mouth!" My mother and I came closer and she was right, Bécassine doesn't have a mouth, not even a line under her nose. We'd never noticed. "Well, that's why she's dumb," Alice concluded, "she can't speak." And she tossed the books under her bed.

Alice's best friend is called Antoine, he has an older brother and two cats. He often comes for sleepovers on the weekend and his parents pick him up on Sunday evening. His father is a teacher, his mother, Nathalie, a lawyer who specializes in women's rights. Rape is her day-to-day world, and she describes terrible incidents of domestic violence. She says women keep coming back to the thing that's killing them, they don't give themselves permission to live. I nod (but perhaps whatever's killing them is their way of living). "That's why we're so happy Antoine gets along well with Alice," she adds. "When boys get together they're already mini men, you know, they have their swords, their pistols, and their super-violent video games, it's crazy. By the time they're eight, they've already scored points on their Game Boys by wasting an enemy. At ten they're watching porn. It's sad really. We have a simple solution—we confiscated his Game Boy. You learn respect right from the start, from childhood, I'm sure of it, the sexes listening to each other, being gentle, peaceful. So, we're real happy he's friends with Alice. Did you know he's always asking to come to your place? He loves it! We—" Alice chooses this moment to burst out of her bedroom into the living room, followed by a bare-chested Antoine with a bandanna around his head, tagatagatagataga, tagatagatagataga, they yell, pelting us with plastic machine guns that I ended up buying for them when they came shopping with me—it's still better than spending the day on Game Boys, I thought, giving in to Alice's pleading, at least they'll be getting some exercise. I lie to Antoine's parents who are rooted to the spot with surprise: "I'm so sorry, it was my father...her grandfather...at Christmas...please forgive him," I add, waving my arms to beg for a cease-fire, "my father's always dreamed of having a boy."

And it's happened now, I think, his dream has come true. And you'll never have another child.

Sometimes I can't take any more, the fear is overwhelming, and I make Alice wear the dresses my mother buys for her. There's one that I would have loved to wear as a child: pale yellow with a flounced hem and a flowery trim on the collar, adorable. Alice refuses, wrinkles her nose, and then puts it on grudgingly. "Take the photo, then I'm taking it off," she says. All at once, she spins around with an incredibly graceful swing of her hips and arms, the flounce flies through the air along with her unbraided hair, she's so gloriously elegant and powerful all at the same time that I'm floored. "Come on, Mom, are you taking this photo?" I do it quickly, my time is tightly rationed. "You could take up dancing, you know, honey, you have a gift, it's blindingly obvious. I used to dance. I loved it. Wouldn't you like that?" She puffs out her cheeks and doesn't answer, she's already peeled off the dress. "Can we play marbles, Momsy?" "Okay, I'm coming."

They'll stay there in an old album, these photos of fashion displays conceded in the name of love, full of pointless dresses that I gaze at from time to time.

One day we're on the RER high-speed subway, just waiting for the train to leave Saint-Michel station, when a punk walks past on the platform with a muzzled, fierce-looking dog on a leash. "Hey, Mom," Alice cries, "look, what's wrong with that dog! He's all red!" I was hoping she wouldn't notice it, but that hope died a death: the pit bull has a violent erection, its thick purplish penis seems to be straining against the leash that hauls at the dog unceremoniously. Disconcerted, I glance at the man sitting opposite us, hoping to get a supportive embarrassed-parent nod or an amused smile. But when I meet his eye—or rather, I don't meet his eyes because he's staring at Alice—his expression betrays the basest human desire I've ever seen in my life (or perhaps once?). I'm helpless. Is this really happening, is it a long-frozen memory that's turning me to water? The man's depraved eyes beam out of his thuggish aging face, oozing raw debauchery, indifference for all humanity, and an offensive disregard for childhood. They communicate cruelty, domination, an unfettered bestial lust, pure malign intent. It's like being at the movies, I don't entirely believe it, assailed by a face up on the screen that is the incarnation of evil—where on earth does a man get an expression like that from, in what far-flung corner of himself? I manage to grab Alice's hand and pull her toward me. "Come on, we're getting off at the next stop." She brushes the man's knee as we pass and the sweet smile she gives him destroys me.

Back at home, I can't find the words to speak to her. I tell her she must watch out for everyone, especially in the street— "Watch out for old people?" she interrupts me. "Yes, of course. But also men, and boys. *Watch out for* as in *don't trust them*. They sometimes want to hurt girls." "I know. They want to catch girls." She doesn't say "catch us." I'm pained to realize she doesn't include herself among the girls. "That's right. And there's no reason why you should let anyone catch you. Your body belongs to you, don't let anyone touch it without a good reason. Do you understand?" "Yes," Alice says, then she adds thoughtfully, "my body belongs to me." "You need to be on the lookout the whole time. Always know who's around you and behind you, know if someone's watching you or following you. Be on the alert but don't make it obvious." "Like the Sioux," she says flattening herself on the carpet. And then I show her the self-defense moves that my father taught Claude and me long ago. "And if you think someone sleazy is following you, put your keys between your fingers to make brass knuckles, with your thumb out like this, and if he attacks you, aim for his face, his eyes, don't even think twice..." She twists her mouth, her whole face changes shape.

The following Sunday I'm working at my desk and I hear Alice tell Antoine, "You take the guy by the shoulders and you bring your knee up hard into his wiener, boom, that'll get rid of him. Your body belongs to you. Geddit?"

We occasionally go to Rouen to visit my parents. Alice is always happy, she loves her grandparents, especially her grandmother. We spend Saturday night at Grandma's house and Sunday with grandpa where she meets Adam, who's her uncle, Elsa points out, amused. "You'll just have to call him Little Uncle, like in Chekhov plays," she tells Alice as a joke, the first time they meet. But I personally hate the word "uncle," and secretly reject it. I keep the word "brother" for myself, like the word "son."

Adam is soon walking and babbling. My father—his father, our father!—is lying on the carpet (he'll struggle to get back up), playing with the Circuit 24 with him, but the toddler's mostly interested in the noise that the remote-controlled race cars make. Alice blocks her ears—I'm delighted to see that she doesn't like cars. But she adores Adam himself—I'm thrilled to see that she likes babies. Perhaps I should have made more of a thing of dolls when she was little, I think. My father turns on the radio while we're having lunch. The presenter Lucien Jeunesse has died but the game show *Le Jeu des 1,000 francs* is still going—unbelievable. On the news a heated argument breaks out between two guests about the rape of a female journalist in Cairo's Tahrir Square. One of them is outraged that Arab countries are being stigmatized when the situation is far from perfect in France. "Do you know that a woman is raped every six minutes in France?" he rails. "Oh, poor thing!" says my father. We laugh. "He'll never change," Elsa champions him, glancing at him tenderly and indulgently.

Alice is now twelve and has moved to junior high. She's reunited with almost all her friends from primary school but the configuration has changed. The schoolyard belongs to the boys and there are now many more of them racing out to play soccer at recess, which means Alice can no longer get a look-in. They all know she's good but they leave her on the touchline, "real sorry." She sometimes joins the game a minute before the bell rings, it's hopeless. When Antoine's parents move, she feels the blow all the more keenly. With no other option, she then befriends a few girls who enjoy roller-skating; at the end of the day they power up and down the boulevard outside school, pounding their arms.

A few days before leaving for Tokyo where her father still lives, Alice decides to cut her bangs to look like Xena the Warrior Princess, her TV heroine who fights monsters, gods, and death itself. She hesitated between Xena and Sydney Fox, the archaeologist admired by her sensible assistant Nigel, Alice tells me, but even though Sydney's good at martial arts, Xena's the best. She takes the kitchen scissors from the drawer early in the morning and, without even looking in a mirror, chops her hair every which way, from memory. She then comes bursting into my bedroom, a little anxious about my reaction but not about the results of her handiwork. "It's horrific," I say, genuinely horrified. She pulls a silly face and does a somersault, but I'm not happy, not happy at all. "You look like nothing on earth," I say. She seems to take this as a compliment.

"We'll have to cut it short, it's the only solution," is the hairdresser's diagnosis. Alice gives a beaming smile. "That's terrible," I say. "Short hair at twelve! She'll look like a boy!" Alice's eyes sparkle. "Not necessarily. I'm a stylist," says the hairdresser, "I'll do something pretty. Look," he adds, swiveling Alice's chair around to face me. "It's all about the balance. In every face there are masculine elements, here and here in Alice's case," he says indicating her chin and nose, "and feminine elements: her eyes and mouth. You just have to choose what you want to emphasize." I look at him. He personally obviously opted for the female angle. As for Alice, she spins her chair straight back toward the mirror and, jutting out her chin, does a talented impersonation of Kirk Douglas.

As the first tufts start to fall, I stand up. "I'm taking a walk around the block," I say. Out on the street I'm unsteady on my feet. My cell beeps, it's a message from my mother. "I'm really thinking of you on this anniversary," her voice quavers. "You're my darling daughter. Big kiss, I love you." I grind to a halt there on the sidewalk. It's today. I'd forgotten. There are only two people left on earth who remember when Tristan was born, when Tristan died. Two people in the whole world. Maybe three, but Christian no longer shows me that sort of consideration. Neither does my mother, usually. But she has today. Her kindness wards off my pain for a moment. A day is like a face: it's all about the balance. But today's also the day that Alice decided to cut her hair, I think to myself. She knows it too, one way or another, she knows what day it is today.

"Here," says the hairdresser, handing me an envelope, "I thought you'd like to keep it." Through the opening I can see a thick lock of fair hair held by a ribbon. I stammer my thanks. What a sweetheart this boy is, I think. Alice is glowing. I hang back slightly on the street to watch. She walks ahead of me with her naked neck, sturdy shoulders, and swinging arms. Her haircut makes her look older. She looks like a fifteen-year-old boy who's just landed from the moon.

At lunchtime a few days later, a Saturday, I come upstairs with the mail in my hand and walk into the apartment. From the corridor I can see someone sitting with their back to me at the kitchen table, he has tousled hair as if he's only just got out of bed, and, dressed in the sort of tank top we used to call a wifebeater, he's leaning over a bowl of cereal, elbows spread wide on the table. I'm so surprised I drop the letters I'm carrying: who's here? I wonder, my heart pounding, as I crouch in the shadows. "Hi, Mom," says Alice without turning around. "Hello, my darling," I say. "Say, you slept late."

Christian sends me a highly critical email from Tokyo. Alice has just had her whatsit for the first time and he had to go buy her some protection from the pharmacy. "Do you think I know how to say 'sanitary towel' in Japanese?" he complains. "You could have planned ahead..." And while he's on the subject, he needs to discuss an important problem. "You've completely given up your role as a mother to your daughter"—*your* daughter, he writes— "that's the bottom line of womanhood. She doesn't watch her figure, she's too muscly, and the way she dresses is terrible. And what the hell is that haircut? Are you doing this on purpose or something?" His message enrages me, but I agree: I've let her get away with too much, I'm a useless mother.

Alice comes home with a suitcase full of presents: a flowery kimono, sequined barrettes, and a My First Makeup Set in a sophisticated lacquered box. "Here,

Mom, these are for you," she says, as she used to with the jewelry Kevin gave her. "No, Alice, those are presents from your father to you. You should put on the kimono and the barrettes, and send him a photo, it will make him happy." She picks up the parcels reluctantly and goes off to her room with a sigh. "Life's no picnic," she says.

From that day on, I'm at her the whole time. I've been too offhand and she's now going through puberty, the tactics are changing, I need to redress the balance. She's been a wannabe boy, now she can become a successful girl. That's my goal.

I buy her pantyhose and ankle boots with a heel. As I watch her gangling like a giraffe calf, I realize she's only ever walked on the flat and only ever worn sneakers. At thirteen, I already had a modest heel on my Mary Janes, even if I did prefer brogues. I gather up all her soccer shirts, frayed from so much wear, and give them to charity. I take her shopping, buy her skirts and dresses, and get angry if she doesn't wear them at least once a week. She balks. "I don't want to look like a nerd," she grumbles but, to my surprise, she concedes. Feeling encouraged, I buy her some day cream, barrettes with ribbons on them, deodorant, and an eau de toilette by Anaïs Anaïs. I constantly tell her she's beautiful, and it's true. When she goes to a birthday party, I suggest she wear a little mascara, there, like that, just a touch, I show her how to look up as she applies it with the wand. With makeup on, her eyes are just sublime, I hope she knows it. Antoine's parents have moved abroad, which suits me fine. Girls start coming to our apartment again, they draw hearts on their diaries and say they're BFFs. I'm pleased to hear them giggle as they talk about boys in their class, making fun of a big heavy boy who offers girls five euros for a kiss. In ninth grade she asks to have her ears pierced, something I've never had done myself. She wears simple, chic little silver hoops. For her fourteenth birthday her friends give her pink nail polish, a braided bracelet, and hair scrunchies. "What a babe," they squeal. They watch the old musical *The Young Girls of Rochefort* and sing along to the tunes by heart. I relax and, to set an example, take more care with what I wear, no longer trailing around in my pajamas all day on Sunday. Everything leads me to believe that my femininity drive is working, even if the sports coach's enthusiasm in Alice's school report (she scores 20/20) slightly dents my conviction: "Exceptional ability in rugby. Well done!" Most likely a throwback from her grandfather... "In my day," I tell Alice, "girls didn't play rugby. It's far too violent." "Well, I love it," she retorts. I let it go, so long as she doesn't have thighs like a scrum half... Luckily, she gets thumped on the nose, which cools her ardor. I couldn't be happier.

One evening we're watching a film that I picked at random from the video club and all of a sudden there's a sex scene. I search frantically for the remote but can't find it so I put my hands over Alice's eyes. "Just stop that, Mom," she says coolly. "I do *know*, you know...Right now she's going to give him a blow job, and there you go." A blow job! I can't breathe. To think I was planning to teach her about sex—I'd been waiting till she was fourteen! But it's already old news from what I can see: Antoine's father may not have liked firearms, but he wasn't averse to using porn sites on the family computer. "Did you watch a lot?" I ask anxiously. "No," she says, "I thought it was so *disgusting*." "But that's not like real life," I protest anxiously. And I make much of how wonderful it can be when two people really love each other, sex, basically, the union of two bodies is a sort of fusion, there's a unique harmony, a man and a woman can be almost...I go over the top, I have no idea where I dig up the romantic images I bombard her with. "Okay, fine, Mom," she says, "but I don't need to hear your life story."

Daniel contacts me on Messenger, he eventually tracked me down on Facebook. "Gorgeous profile picture," he says. He tells me he's accepted that I don't want to see him again, but he's been thinking about our conversation on that Rouen–Paris train and he has a suggestion for me. Of course, I can turn it down (but no, I don't want to). So here it is: the partnership of psychologists that he works with in court is arranging an international study day on incest and he thought I could contribute a sort of witness statement in order to provide a different angle, something less didactic and more sensitive. He's sure it won't be easy for me, but it might do me good to talk about it. Maybe. "It's in Nice, you could bring your swimsuit…" he adds. Swimming far out to sea now strikes me as such a simple longing that can be realized, and there's something comforting about the thought.

My mother agrees to come and look after Alice while I'm away, so long as it doesn't eat into her choir days—she's discovered she has a fine contralto voice and is preparing for a nationwide tour with her singing group. "What will you be doing in Nice?" she asks on the phone. "Is it for work?" "Not really," I say. "I'm going to a symposium on incest." "On incest? Will you be translating?" "No, Mom. I'll be there as a contributor." The pause is furnished with imperceptible static. "But what's your connection with that?" she asks eventually.

"Thank you so much for your contribution, it was very interesting. You said you still have nightmares crawling with cockroaches, ants, and spiders," one psychoanalyst says at the end of the symposium. "Has it ever occurred to you that insect is an anagram of incest?" Yet another try-hard word game, just like all the other shrinks, I think to myself while he confidently develops his point. I mean, I can't see where this is going, but he thought I was interesting, so I smile. Besides, Daniel was right, talking did me good. I should have done it sooner—consulted a professional, "seen someone," as people say. But where would that have gotten me? Daniel chaired the interview today, he helped me, but I can't really see myself pouring out my story to a stranger. Keep dirty laundry in the family. Daniel is in the audience, he smiles at me. We may yet end up making love, I think to myself.

Alice lets her hair grow again. She's tired of making constant trips to the hairdresser to keep her short style in line, she hates going there. But she also hates being called "young man" in shops when she wears pants—and I don't like it when people say "Good morning, sir, ma'am," when we're together. She watches as her hair slowly grows back, infuriated by different length layers that make her look such a mess, and she adjusts her barrettes in the mirror. "You see," my mother says, "I told you she'd get over her boyish phase. Your sister was the same, back in the day..."

My triumph is modest and all-embracing. I'm so reassured that I never comment when she arm wrestles boys, comes home with 20/20 in shot put, or drops a casual "suck my balls" into conversation, it doesn't make any sense, but it actually sounds kind of funny coming from a girl, I tell myself—not very refined, but funny. "Mind you," my mother adds, "this is when the trouble starts. After puberty, girls are always more difficult than boys..." And I do start to understand my father's fears all those years ago. "Would you like me to make a gynecologist appointment for you?" I ask. Alice shakes her head, she'll go when she feels like it, she knows what to do, she's not a moron.

She does have a boyfriend, though; I was thrilled to catch them kissing under the front porch one time. Alice doesn't answer my matronly questions, she hardly even deigns to tell me he's Tunisian and she met him at tennis class. She dumps him a few weeks later. He was always asking her what she did when they weren't together, it drove her nuts, she says. Plus he couldn't stand the fact that she wiped the floor with him in tennis. "That macho idiot can suck my balls," she concludes.

She's organizing a big party at home for her fifteenth birthday and has asked me to be out, to go to a midnight movie. "No alcohol," I tell her. "Of course," she promises. She borrows my white and pink dress and puts on high-heeled sandals. She has legs like a gazelle, I'm proud of how beautiful she is, when I was her age I didn't show off my legs enough, I didn't make the most of them, I should have. When I arrive home, I can hear the music thudding through the open windows, the neighbors must be furious. In the hallway a bare-chested young man tears down the stairs, almost knocks me over, and hollers, "Hi, ma'am," his breath loaded with vodka. He must be eighteen or twenty, very good-looking. How strange, I think, there's another party going on in the building on the same day. Then I realize he's come from my apartment, and I don't dare go home, I stay out on the landing on the floor below, paralyzed by shyness, or shame, I can't be sure; I feel happy and sad at the same time. "That was Corentin," Alice explains. "He plays guitar in a band." I take off my makeup in the bathroom. "Your little girl's grown up," the mirror tells me.

When she's in eleventh grade, Alice does her guided project on women and feminism. "You know the worst thing, Mom, women have always been scared the whole time, all over the world and all through the ages. Obviously they're not so scared here as in India or some other places, but still, consciously or not, they live in fear, fear of men." I put down my knife next to the little pile of peelings, and wipe my hands. "That's true, my darling. But men are scared too. Does it really have to be us against them? Couldn't—" "It's totally different. Domination comes from men. Okay, so some of them may be scared, but we don't need to waste any tears on them. If not, why did you teach me to defend myself when I was a kid? Do you remember, wham bam?" She mimes the up-thrust of a knee. "It's because you were scared for me. Because all women are scared, period. It's so normal, they so completely interiorized the danger that some of them don't even realize, but...saying a 'threatened woman' is tautological." "Good point. But being scared of never measuring up, scared of getting it wrong, not succeeding, failing—that affects men too, right? You girls these days, you're so..." Alice jumps up, hurls the peeled potatoes into the water, and, still with the peeler in her hand, says in a voice shaking with emotion, "So, Mom, the difference between men and women is that men are scared for their honor but women are scared for their lives. Making a fool of yourself doesn't kill you, but violence does." I get to my feet, I know this, I put my arms around her, "hug," she says. When she was little, I could pick her up as if there was nothing to her, bowled over by how light she was. I was so powerful! I can't do that now, or walk around the apartment like a robot with her feet on top of mine. Her cell phone rings, she hurries out of the kitchen with a seductive "hello." I hum as I set the table. I think Alice is too radical and uncompromising, but our conversation made me happy, we're talking together, one girl to another, I think to myself.

"Am I disturbing you, Mom?" Alice asked, coming into my bedroom. "No, honey, never," I said without turning around, my eyes glued to my computer screen. She stood behind me and patted the top of my head. "I wanted to let you know I'm going out this evening." She left a pause, for the third time I deleted the sentence I'd been toiling over for fifteen minutes. "And I may not come home for the whole weekend," she added.

I broke off from what I was doing, spun around in my chair, and looked up at her, "What did you say?" She sat down on my bed. "Are you going to Isa's house?" Isa is a friend from high school whose parents have a house in Étretat; Alice has been there several times. "No," she said, "not Isa. It's someone you don't know." "And this is how you tell me this, at the last minute?" I asked her mischievous little smile—rebellious, actually, I thought, that was the word for it, the best possible translation: a rebellious little smile, impish but slightly insolent too, with a nugget of revolt wrapped in appealing cheerfulness. "How do you want me to tell you?" she said, lying full length on my bed, with her arms flung slackly on either side of her head, in the same position of abandon as a sleeping baby, a position she's never lost. "I don't know, that's just it. You're very mysterious. Which tells me something's going on." "Maybe." She now had her feet pointing at the ceiling and was doing a shoulder stand. "Well?" She smiled. "Wait, let me guess," I said. "You're in love?" She waggled her hands and feet like a happy puppet. Meanwhile my brain was accelerating at the same rate as my heartbeat. (Here we go, it's happening. Is she on the pill? Have I explained everything to her properly? Are the condoms that I bought last year still usable? And she has her French exam for her baccalaureate in a month...) She was sitting back up now, still giving me the same mocking smile but not answering. "You're in love and you want to stay the night at his place, is that it?" She half opened her mouth, a shadow flitted over her eyes, a bird in flight. "Come on, then, tell me," I said holding out my hand, and she took it. "What's his name?" With one finger she smoothed the vein on my wrist, a vein that's been prominent for a while now, and she stayed like that with her head lowered, then looked up at me. "Mom," she said. "Yes," I replied, "I'm here." She smiled at me—and when she smiles like that, she's radiant, I can't put it any other way, she's like a sun—"The thing is…" She stopped, her voice left hanging, as if held back behind her lips, then she gave me a little pat on the back and, every inch of her glowing with light, she said, "It's a girl."

EPILOGUE

You can't say you're stunned, even if you are—you are in the true sense of the word that you learned long ago in a French lesson: it's from the Old French word *estoner*, thunderstruck, and you're thunderstruck. What shocks you is the way things happen, this sort of chain of events and you feel you're the weak link, perhaps even the vital missing part. But you don't use the word "shock" much since seeing it in Tristan's medical files, *death by respiratory shock.* The image has never left you, the material quality of its literal meaning: the astonishment of a baby whose heart stops, the surprise of death on the cusp of life. There are words that carry curses within them, you have every reason to know that. Your astonishment takes your breath away too, time is a boulder that you're hauling up a hill and it tumbles back down. You're trying to understand but you don't know what. What is there to understand? You're in foreign territory, in a country whose language you don't speak. You can't translate it, it's too far removed from you, from what you know. Perhaps it's your pride that's hurting you: You've failed to alter the course of things, life keeps going, heading its own sweet way without you, you never determined any of it. You're hypnotized by colorful arabesques on your computer screen, in a daze. A childhood memory resurfaces, don't ask why. There were dozens of rabbit cages in the courtyard overlooked by the bedroom that you shared with your sister—in Rouen? Yes, right in the middle of Rouen. Early in the morning, before the pigeons stirred, you could hear them shaking their big ears in their cramped enclosures. You weren't allowed to go and feed them, the yard was locked. Many years went by before you asked what those rabbits were for, you may well have been afraid you'd be told they were used to make stew. Then one day they all disappeared. No more cages, no more noises, nothing. That was when you asked the question, and your father replied, he knew the answer, obviously. The rabbits belonged to the medical analysis laboratory on the second floor of the building, and they were used for pregnancy tests. To find out whether a woman was pregnant, her urine was injected into a rabbit's back. If she was pregnant, your father explained, the pregnancy hormones in her urine would make the rabbit's ovaries swell—in female rabbits, naturally, but that goes without saying. And how did they know that the rabbit's ovaries had swollen? By killing them, of course, dummy. All those disemboweled rabbits broke your heart on the spot, the mental picture with all that red hounded you almost to the point of suffocation. You asked your mother whether it had been thanks to a rabbit that she'd known she was expecting you, but she didn't really listen to or didn't really understand the question because she replied absently "You did, my bunny rabbit" and you swore to yourself that you'd never have any children. Why is this memory here now? You don't know. You're creating a diversion. You can't concentrate now so you shut down your computer, feeling a little nauseous. Alice pops her head around the door, ready to leave. "Mom?" "Yes?" "I love you too."

There will be the evening when she comes home in tears from the demonstrations in favor of marriage for everyone, and you won't know what to do. An old man spat at her as she passed him, calling her a bitch, she watched spellbound as his spittle dribbled down her jacket—"a man who could have been my grandpa," she'll say, and her sixteen-year-old anguish will be so sharp that tears will form in your own eyes. There will be your father's seventy-fifth birthday when you ask her to wear a touch of mascara for the occasion and in the train on the way there you'll tell her, "Don't talk about it, it's better that way." And seeing her sad expression you'll quickly explain, "He wouldn't understand." (But do you even understand?) There will be that time when your father gets Adam to blow out his birthday candles and then starts fulminating about the demonstrators who stopped him taking his son to soccer the day before—"Faggots and dykes are such a pain in the ass," he'll say by way of summary. You'll look at Alice, sense her hesitation, but she won't say anything and you'll be inexpressibly relieved, you'd rather no one knew, you don't want her to tell anyone. Nothing really exists until it has been said out loud, you know that from experience, there may be an element of mutilation to this policy, but there's the salvation of forgetting too, you'll think. And then there'll be your mother leafing through *Paris Match* at the hairdresser and recognizing her granddaughter under a placard saying "I want a divorce too," and then you won't be able to deny it, first, because it was your mother who knitted her the red cap she's wearing in the picture, but second, because she borrowed some black duct tape from you to make her placard, and the slogan did make you laugh, even though you were worried. "Oh, she'll get over it," your mother will predict. "She'll get over it before I go back to it. I had a little thing with a girl too, when I was seventeen. My friend Paulette," she adds to your amazement. "You don't really know what you want at that age, you try things, test the water, then you get over it."

Then the day will come—you'll hate yourself but it will be too late, you won't be able to stop your fear escalating—the day will come when you sit down facing Alice who...Yes, I remember. Wait, let me finish. Why don't we talk about when she was born?

I sit down facing Alice who's typing away on her phone in the living room, I look at her, her long blond hair is waist-length, she's wearing a T-shirt with the words "Little Cutie" on it, she's just turned seventeen, she's beautiful. "You know something, Alice, I sometimes think it's because of me." She doesn't look up, just answers halfheartedly "What is, Mom?" and keeps typing. I clear my throat. "Yes, I think I didn't know how to go about it, didn't succeed in passing on to you what, well, a mother's role should be toward her daughter, I think, teaching her, guiding her, passing on a liking for, for, for womanhood." She looks up at this word, the solemn clarity of her expression piercing right through me. "Mom. Why are you telling me this?" "No, darling, it's just that when I see how pretty you are without makeup, without anything, I think you could be, well, I think I must have messed something up when you were a child, I don't know, something I wasn't any good at, that must be it. It's all my fault." She straightens, stares at me unblinkingly, shrewdly, I can see my curved reflection in her blue iris. "Why your fault? What fault, Mom? When you say it's your fault and you're guilty, that means there's an offense, a crime. What exactly is the offense here, Mom?" "You know what I mean..." I don't dare hold her eye, I stammer, I'm ashamed, but when I look up at her again, her eyes have already forgiven me, I can see love happen right there in front of me, unconditional: her eyes forgive me. "Here's an example: I'm thinking about Tristan. I never should have talked to you about him. You wanted to take his place, you didn't feel loved enough, you—" "And so that's why I'm a lesbian, as you see it? Is that the offense?" The word "lesbian" knocks the breath out of me, but then the other words are unbearable, dyke, butch, even homosexual, I have to admit that I struggle to hear it said, to utter it myself, I can't get used to it. "Two things, Mom," Alice says (oh, but the happiness when she says "Mom," the blazing happiness every single time). "First of all, you don't know anything about it. Maybe I would be straight if Tristan didn't die, but maybe I wouldn't. I might not be here, or I might be. Either way, we already talked about this: people don't choose their sexuality, they don't decide, do you get that? There's no point saying it's down to this or down to that, a result of, because of, I should have, etc. It just is. Period." "Yes, of course, my darling, I just wanted to make the point that there were circumstances that, well, it was a pity." Alice stiffens. "A pity? But what is this, Mom? What's the problem?" "Well, sometimes it stresses me, I wonder...do you think you'll ever fall in love with a boy? Is it impossible?" She shrugs, she's tiring of this conversation. "I don't know. Maybe. Nothing's impossible. There are boys I think are hot, but...people fall in love with a person—boy or girl—it's the person they love, not a thing, not a gender. So, in theory, I won't rule it out but…And anyway, I'm with Sophie, can I remind you. I'm very happy with her. We love each other."

I should stop there, I should shut my mouth, but it's as if I need to purge myself of a deep, age-old fear, something ancient, deep-rooted, and all-consuming, like swarming insects, like stinking stained hands gripping hold of me and forcing their way in. "Well then," I keep going, and it's almost an exclamation, "will you never make love with a boy?" She laughs her mocking laugh and it gives me courage to go on. "Not even to try? That really would be a pity." She looks at me kindly, with a little undertone of taunting, and she stretches. "How about you, Mom, have you ever made love with a girl? Even just to *try*?" I shake my head, rolling my eyes, whatever next. I laugh to brush aside my embarrassment, and hers too perhaps. "So you see. Why should I *try* when no one's ever told you that you should?"

What to say? As I reach over the coffee table for my cigarettes, I drop my lighter. I bend to pick it up. The sun suddenly beams through the window in a break in the clouds. It's almost as if there's an angel in the room. We sit in silence and Tristan goes to sit at the far end of the sofa, gently enveloping us—his sister and me—with his presence, then he disappears just as gently. Alice finishes writing her text, and looks at me again, she's weighing something up, thinking. Her face has a translucent beauty, it shows all the unadulterated power of her innocence, her fundamental inability to do harm, destroy, or hate, her impishness.

"You know, Mom..." she picks up the conversation—she enunciates clearly and, amusingly, there's a teacherly note in her voice—"you know, a girl's nice too. And even," she smiles as if at a memory, "it's wonderful, a girl's wonderful."

Sometimes just one sentence can bring monuments crashing down. Dungeons of terror, ramparts of shame and towers collapse, places where you were once prisoner and jailer, and all at once they're filled with sunlight, you're through with those meager arrow-slit windows. The crisp air fills your lungs, it grates and then leaves again, and even though the light is bright, you're not blinded. All it takes is one sentence, hardly even that, a word, an adjective left as a blank in an incomplete sentence, a little something that was missing, that was so painfully absent and she, Alice, has just gently set it down where it belongs, just like that, and suddenly the world opens up, a new meaning hatches in your mouth, you disembark, and you're in wonderland. And then there's only one thing you can do, and I did it: you have to take the sentence and claim it, save it, repeat the password, hand it on, and never forget it.

"You're right, my darling," I said. "A girl's wonderful."

CREDITS

Camille Laurens is an award-winning French novelist and essayist. She received the Prix Femina, one of France's most prestigious literary prizes, in 2000 for *Dans ces bras-là*, which was published in the United States as *In His Arms* in 2004. Her previous books include *Who You Think I Am* (Other Press, 2017) and *Little Dancer Aged Fourteen* (Other Press, 2018). She lives in Paris.

Adriana Hunter studied French and Drama at the University of London. She has translated more than ninety books, including Véronique Olmi's *Bakhita* and Hervé Le Tellier's *Eléctrico W*, winner of the French-American Foundation's 2013 Translation Prize in Fiction. She lives in Kent, England.